Star of Hidden Skies

Volume Three of the Trilogy
Journeys To Lost Landscapes

Dallin Chapman

Newman Books

First published in Great Britain in 2019

By
Newman Books
45 Shipston Road
Stratford-upon-Avon
Warwickshire
CV37 7LN

Printed and bound in the UK by G H Smith & Son, The Advertiser Office, Market Place, Easingwold, York, YO61 3AB

ISBN 978-0-9558699-7-6

For Peter

HEDRON

NATHAN

GALAN

ANNA

TORAN

JANE

SOLACE

ELLEN — JORRAN'S DAUGHTER

EDWARD — TORAN'S GRANDSON

{ SIMON — TORAN'S SON
{ CATHERINE " J.I. LAW

{ LACHLAN — TORAN'S
{ JOCQUELA   GRANDCHILDREN

{ SHAYRATH — BROTHERS — SH LOOKED AFTER THEIR MOTHER.
{ ETHAN   ETH IN ARMY BUT GOT DISMISSED

JOSIAH — CARPENTER WHO TURNS UP TO HELP CARVE THE TREE

iv

The Summons

Viewed from far out in the depths the globe looked beautiful, a turning ball of blue and silver, dancing to the beat of countless other worlds. The people who walked its ways did not know that it was being observed, watched through eyes unclosed since the beginning, nor did they comprehend the magnitude of what was happening, that its grandeur was fading and gaping scars marred its once pure skin. Intent upon the day-to-day, the custodians took its wealth of treasures as infinite, running up and down the avenues of their time and plundering the golden wells.

The globe hung like a dying creature, spurred to ever greater feats of endurance. The people did not feel the watching eyes, unblinking in their unending vigil, nor did they notice how, imperceptibly, the distant planets seemed to draw closer. They heard the far off thunder and dismissed it as irrelevant; they saw the changing patterns of their little kingdom and did not realise that the hour was fast approaching when they would have to decide.

The watcher stirred and, all across the open spaces, the summons rang for the gathering in to begin.

Abiding with Hope

There was a stirring in the atmosphere that breathed of change. The people continued to live out the rhythm of their lives but, as time passed, and sunset sank into the twilight of evening day upon day, they sensed movement that seemed part of the very air itself, and of the land they walked upon.

Going to their work in forests, fields, schools and the many places that sustained their community, collecting the daily food and sharing it with family and those who might otherwise eat alone, all this they faithfully continued. Yet, when they stood together in the Centre of Worship before the ancient table carved with the flow of seasons, the life of their people, and raised their arms to sing, longing for the Tree filled their hearts with increasing intensity, and the yearning to walk again to the shelter of its branches.

Hedron and Nathan were silent as they took their evening journey to the edge of the dwellings. Above, the sky was a rich velvet ablaze with stars, and the moon hung over them, its white light guiding their footsteps.

It was not until they stood gazing into the distance, to the way passing amongst woods, along undulating pathways, and through the valley of slender trees, the way they had travelled before but now could only see in the quiet fastness of memory, that Hedron spoke.

"Nathan, the time is come when we must speak together, and then we will call a meeting of all the Counsellors"

"Yes, Hedron. I know."

"Do you remember what I said when we last talked about this, what I felt, the Great Tree...?"

"I remember. You said that one day we would be able to

make that journey again, that the Tree still rises up in the middle of the plain, holding out its arms in invitation to all who will come as we did before, to rest against its ancient breast, its renewing bark."

Hedron smiled and placed his hand on the young Counsellor's arm.

"Yes, you remember. And I also said that I believe the time will come when all peoples will be drawn to the heart of its centre."

"You said that too. I often meditate upon those words."

The two men spoke no more for a while, but let the magnificence of evening unfold its mystery before them. At last, Nathan turned to Hedron, his face pale in the moonlight.

"The new star we noticed some time ago, it seems to be drawing closer and growing brighter. What can it mean?"

"We may not ask, Nathan. We can only wait until the knowledge is given to us."

"You said once that you felt the patterns of creation were stirring and that, somewhere, Galen and Anna are part of that mystery."

Hedron looked at the younger man, tall and fine like his father, his tumbling curls white in the moonlight. He remembered the ten year-old boy who had come running to him in distress when Galen and Anna disappeared.

"There is movement amongst the spheres. We can only be patient."

"But there will be a calling in and a final consolation?"

"That is what I feel, but I do not understand." Hedron turned his gaze from the sky with reluctance. "Let us go and continue the unchanging rhythm of our days until..."

"Until we may return to the Tree," murmured Nathan.

In the far distance they could see light streaming above the

Centre of Worship whilst, all around them, the constellations drew countless patterns across the deep. In all the nobility of night, the unknown star was more sharply defined than any other, shining with increasing radiance and drawing ever closer as they walked.

Chapter 1

Toran had been drawing for hours, pausing at intervals to survey his work, sighing frequently at his inability to create on paper the vision in his head. He did not notice the fading light until he could no longer make out the detail on the page. He stood up then and stretched, tired and stiff after hours of sitting hunched over the table. Outside his cottage window he could see the first faint etching of the moon and, beyond it, a single star hanging in the twilight.

He was quite alone. At such times the cottage closed around him like a cage, and he felt its silence as a malign presence, daring him to fill the empty spaces with sounds of life. He walked towards the television and hesitated; it would be all talk of the possibility of war. He had heard it so many times he knew the script by heart. If it did come, probably he would not survive. If it did not, then at seventy the time must arrive when the battle within his own body would dominate any external force. It was not himself he was concerned about; meanwhile, he had work to do. Until he fulfilled his task, there would be no rest for him.

He went into the hall and opened the front door onto the village street. The few lamps along the road were already lit, and the surrounding houses and cottages looked welcoming with their glowing windows. Toran breathed deeply, relaxing as the country air filled his lungs, marvelling at the healing power of the natural world all around him. The scents and sounds of early summer flooded through him and he felt ashamed of his earlier moment of self-pity, his sense of isolation. He knew he was not alone. He would go to bed and get some much-needed rest.

He was up early the next morning, awake even as the first light nudged at his window. Following the death of his wife he had rarely slept late, but since he had been looking for the right place to build upon, his sense of urgency and excitement drove him from his bed long before most people in the village were stirring. He pondered as he stood in the kitchen drinking his tea. The feelings of the previous evening had evaporated, and he was filled with a sense of anticipation and hope. Perhaps today he would discover what he was searching for.

Shutting the front door quietly behind him, he glanced up and down the street: empty except for his neighbour's cat sidling back from a night's hunting. He walked quickly along the deserted road until he reached the church. He loved the ancient building and came here often, sometimes sitting inside for hours lost in contemplation, or resting on the secluded bench close to Jane's grave, where he could taste the sea breeze and look at the countryside over the stone wall.

Today, he stood for a few moments and absorbed the peace that always swept over him when he approached. The tower glinted in the early morning sun, and the clock face seemed to stare down at him in recognition. The hand slipped to six, and the striking of the hour rang out. For some reason, the sound struck him as never before; there seemed something in the note of the chime that was different. He shook his head, puzzled, and looked at the sky beyond. In the east, the sun was brightening and, with a start of surprise, he saw high above his head the same star he had noticed the night before from his cottage window. It was unusual to see one so clearly at this time of day. He searched for the fading moon, but could not find it.

Toran threw back his head and breathed deeply. The clock

had finished striking, but the notes trembled in his ears still and voiced his deepest longing: today, you will find the place upon which to build the sanctuary.

At seventy, Toran was still a fine looking man. Tall and broad-shouldered, no aging stoop marred his step, and his abundance of silver hair had long been a talking point in the village. He had lived there for fifteen years now, moving from the city in an instinctive rejection of the kind of life he felt forced to live there. Jane had felt the same. During their ten years in the cottage, they tried to find a different and kinder way. They had expected to contribute all they could as part of a small community, and thus experience a sense of homecoming; what they had not anticipated was that, although this had happened, the longer they lived distanced from the changing mores of city existence, the smaller they felt in a much larger world, less significant in a place laden with meaning.

When Jane died, his grief had been almost unbearable, yet he knew he had been left behind to fulfil some unknown task. The idea first took hold of him soon after he noticed the star and, once it had entered his thoughts, he could not dismiss it, carrying his dream like a hidden treasure, and contemplating it with a full and fearful heart.

It was going to be a glorious day. The air was saturated with scents of early summer, whilst the sounds of morning made a vast cathedral of the sky. Toran was climbing steadily up the cliff path, content for the moment to delight in the scene before him. As he ascended from the bay, he could see waves breaking onto the rocks below, surging into the inlets to darken the cliffs. In the distance, the island gleamed in the light. If he had been younger he would have started to run; instead he expressed his exhilaration by waving his arms above his head and clapping his hands together.

At last he paused for breath, dropping to the grass with a sigh of relief, where he lay watching the gulls float past and the occasional white clouds build their sunlit palaces. After a while he sat up and looked at the path ahead. He knew each step, each undulation. He was foolish to return so frequently to this same spot; he should extend his search – and yet, such a thought seemed both exhausting and without hope.

Suddenly he started. He thought he had glimpsed something coming towards him, some speck that seemed more than a large tuft of grass or one of the rocks that lay scattered on the hillside. He had never encountered any other person at this time of the morning, and there were no sheep near this stretch of the cliff. Toran rubbed his eyes. Although he still could not identify it, he was certain now that some living creature was intent upon reaching him. He felt its sense of purpose, a determination that rebutted all denial.

Almost without knowing what he was doing, he rose to his feet, a tremor clutching the back of his throat. Nothing else had changed; the sea still surged below him and, in the distance, the island rose out of the water in turret upon turret of silver rock. All around, the landscape was empty of any human life. Toran held his hand to shield his eyes and gazed more intently, half contemplating whether to retrace his steps down the cliff path.

A few moments later he started to laugh, throwing back his head in amusement at his own cowardice. What he had started to imagine fell away as the familiar and reassuring form of a sheepdog came clearly into view, then walked up to stand in front of him as if it did not intend to go any further. Toran bent to touch the head that brushed against his knees.

"You'd best be off back home, my friend; someone will be looking for you."

The animal looked at him with patient eyes and did not stir. It must be from one of the farms that stood further inland, but it was strange that such a dog should leave its duties and set off across the fields on its own. Yet Toran sensed that no command or cajoling from him would persuade it to leave.

"I'm off then."

He set his face once more towards the cliff top and the path that ascended towards its summit. He did not look down as he climbed but, as if they were one body, the dog moved with him.

He had no idea how long he had been walking, for he had left his watch behind. From the height of the sun in the sky, he guessed it must be about ten o'clock, yet he felt as if unfathomable hours had passed since he stood beneath the church clock as it struck the sixth hour. He had taken a short rest on a couple of occasions and, once, he must have nodded off because he came to with a start and lay wondering where he was. The dog was still with him, close by his side, neither leading nor trailing behind, rather moving beside him as if they had planned some itinerary together and were agreed upon their destination. Despite his rests, Toran was growing weary. In his rucksack were sandwiches and a bottle of water. He would eat and drink, then decide what to do.

"I'm afraid I have nothing much for you," he said to his companion, proffering a little ham, pouring some water into the cup he always carried, but the animal seemed disinterested and sat upon the grass at his side unmoving.

They had passed a couple of farmhouses as they travelled, far away to the right, squat and sturdy against the gales which swept this coast in winter. Toran had half expected

9

the dog to leave him then, to hear a shout of ownership that called it away. But no such voice came, nor did the creature give the slightest sign that other forces beckoned. Toran was pleased. There was something about the presence of the dog that gave him some reassurance and comfort; if he had been on his own, he would have been feeling increasingly concerned.

He had lost his sense of direction. He knew such a thing was not possible for the path was the only one and clearly defined but, in some inexplicable way, he must have wandered off his route. He had reached the rocky summit, pausing to look at the ocean far below him, noting, as he always did, the circle of stones on the promontory in the distance, the caves along the rocky coastline beyond which the dolphins often played. He had set off from there with confident steps, the dog close by his side, and it was not until he had looked ahead and realised that he could not see the stone circle that he had hesitated. Instinctively he had turned his gaze out to sea, but the island was shrouded in mist, and only the constantly moving water met his eyes.

Toran chewed his sandwich slowly. He must be more tired than he realised. He had covered this path so many times; if he stayed near the edge of the cliff he would soon see familiar landmarks. And yet…

"What do you think, my friend?" he said to his companion, but the animal made no response, sitting like a statue as if it had not registered his voice, as if it were listening to something else. Toran heard it then – the unmistakable cry of an animal in distress. He rose to his feet, dropping the half-finished sandwich, looking around trying to identify the direction from which the sound came. The dog had not stirred, but Toran knew that it listened intently.

"It's a lamb, it must be; lost, strayed away from its mother, or injured." A strange sensation was sweeping over him, an indefinable sadness. He rubbed his eyes and felt a shudder run through his body. The dog had risen to its feet and stood close by Toran's side, the glossy coat brushing against his hand. Toran felt warmth flooding his heart, and the moment of grief passed. He smiled.

"I shall call you Solace, because that is what you are."

The cry came again, urgent and compelling in its plea for help. The breeze seemed to carry the plaintive call all around them, across the clifftop towards the fields, and at the same time out across the waves, as if the little one rode upon their crests and called for rescue. Solace uttered a small whimper, and Toran knew that the dog was waiting to lead him somewhere. Hastily picking up his rucksack, he took a step forward to indicate that he was ready to follow. Without hesitation, the dog walked away from the cliff edge towards a large bush of gorse just above them, beyond which the ground dropped steeply and a small path could be seen winding downwards, spiralling back towards the sea. Surefooted and certain, Solace began to descend and Toran followed, slipping sometimes on the narrow track, hearing now and then the unmistakable bleat of the lamb below. He was just beginning to fear that they would end up above a precipice, that he would be in danger of falling to the rocks below, when they turned a corner and there, silent before him, was the vision of his waking hours and the tapestry of his dreams.

"This is the place!"

As if carved out and created by giant hands, a huge grass plateau lay encircled on three sides by towering cliffs, a vast arena that had been waiting since the beginning for this hour, silent and hidden amongst ancient rocks, undiscovered from the sea, untrodden by footsteps from the land. Many wingspans beneath, the sea swept out to the far horizon where the sky tumbled into its waters in curtains of blue and silver. And rising out of the sea like a jewel fallen from the sun's crown, was the island.

Toran fell to his knees, overcome with rapture. He had found the place to build a sanctuary.

Chapter 2

Solace and the lamb stood side by side, motionless, small figures in the immense amphitheatre of the ocean, whilst Toran paced up and down gazing in wonder at the sight: the level ground, the batallions of cliffs, the isolation. It was clear why he had not discovered it before, nor heard rumours about its existence from the locals. Yet it was curious that such a place lay waiting until now to be found, holding its secret through untold time.

The lamb's cry caught at his heart and he started, realising he had almost forgotten what had led him there. To his shame, Toran saw that the dog stood close to the small creature, guarding it, waiting for him to take notice. He walked rapidly across to the animals and his sense of mortification deepened. The eyes that looked at him held no accusation, yet he could see mirrored there a patience that made his own behaviour seem self-centred and childish. He dropped to his knees beside the lamb, which was silent now and showed no fear.

At first glance there appeared nothing wrong with it. Tentatively, Toran stretched out his hand and touched the white coat. The little creature trembled but did not shy away. Deftly he examined the small, fragile body, whilst the dog stood by his side watching. There was nothing amiss to be found.

"You're alright, little one. You must have lost your mother somehow, though how you found this place is a mystery." He glanced towards the cliff edge, which lay some distance in front of him, then stood up and walked over to within a couple of strides from the precipice. He looked down cautiously at the waves sweeping onto the rocks far below.

No broken body met his eyes, no battered heap of wool and bones lay beneath. Toran shook his head and went back to where the two animals rested side by side, quietly awaiting him. He thought of the miles he had walked earlier and the sheep far away across the fields.

"Where's your mother?"

The lamb gazed at him with limpid eyes and nestled closer to Solace.

Toran stood and stared around with increasing awe. The space seemed to be expanding even as he looked, so that the grasses spun away in swathes of green, dotted with wild flowers, and the sea was merely a distant sigh, the sky an unending dome of blue and silver.

He must return home and begin to make plans, consider his drawings in the light of this discovery. He had lost all track of the hour, but it must be getting late, and he had to find the path he had lost. How would he manage all he had to do, and would he have the strength to carry the lamb back up the cliff, for he would not dare let the little creature attempt such a feat. He could not abandon it. Bending down, he lifted the small body and held it in his arms. He expected it to struggle but, to his surprise, it lay against his chest like a child and looked at him through eyes full of trust.

Solace had been waiting all this time, but now he set off without a command towards the narrow path which wound its way back up the cliff. Toran followed close behind, the wool of the little creature pressed warm against his own jumper, its tiny head against his neck. Frightened that he might slip, he climbed slowly, his breathing laboured with the steepness of the ascent, but at last the gorse bush was there above them, hiding the entrance to the plateau and, a few moments later, they were at the top.

Toran set down the lamb and stood wondering what to do. He couldn't take it all the way back to the village, but would it survive out here on its own? He couldn't see any farm in the distance now, and had no idea in which direction he should go to find one. And, without warning, the weather had changed. Large drops of rain were starting to fall on his head, and he knew that before long there would be a downpour; he must set off home. But the lamb – how could he leave it here alone, risking death from exposure or accident? Surely it must be starving? Perhaps its mother would find it when he was gone; she might be waiting somewhere not far away to reclaim her lost offspring.

At that moment he noticed a rough stone building, low, with no windows, behind a drystone wall a little way from the top of the cliff. It seemed like a miracle, for it offered protection from the rain and wind, and the wall provided a barrier to the cliffs. As if he understood Toran's thoughts, Solace nudged the small animal towards the wall and there Toran lifted the lamb once more and scrambled over. The shelter was dry despite its dilapidated appearance, and there was even some hay on the floor in the corner. He set down the lamb, and it stood gazing at him without moving. He would have to go and hope that it didn't follow. There was nothing else he could do. He was starting to feel exhausted and he had many miles to walk. He would return to the spot early the next morning.

"Come on, Solace."

He started to take the first steps, but the dog remained standing beside the lamb as though he were the master and Toran the one who must obey. For a moment Toran felt almost foolish, as if he had said something out of place, as if he had misunderstood, and that wisdom rested with the animal, that heard what he said, but had quite other plans.

The rain was getting heavier and the wind was rising. Toran started to shiver.

"Come on, old boy," he urged, and tried to place his hand

on Solace's head and lead him away, but the animal pushed its head against Toran's knees as if prompting him to move without him.

He could have wept with sadness and fear. How could he leave like this, and how would he find his way home? Solace had guided him here and, without the dog, how would he retrace his steps? Reluctantly, he climbed back over the wall and stood on the cliff top. He saw the path then, leading along the tops, sloping down towards where the village nestled beside the sea. Relief swept over him.

"I'll be back, I promise you. Look after the lamb."

He walked as fast as possible, head bowed against the sheeting rain, and the wind which sliced across the cliffs and moaned in his ears. His heart was racing with hope and anxiety, but he had found the place for the sanctuary and there would be a way, however impossible that seemed at the moment. He did not look back but, if he had done so, he would have seen Solace standing on the skyline gazing after him, as if he were watching over his steps until he could be seen no more.

Toran did not draw the curtains in his cottage that evening. He felt restless and excited, and he wanted to sense the sky outside and the worlds stretching beyond his own fragile planet. He paced through the small rooms of the cottage, images of the grassy plateau in his head, and he imagined the foundation stones being laid and the building rising higher and higher, the doors wide open, immense in their welcome.

The time had come to call for the others. He hurried to his desk and took out pen and paper, pausing for a moment as he considered what he must say. His computer lay in front of him, but such important words were too significant to be trusted to the vagaries of the technical age.

The rain had cleared. Glancing outside, he saw the stranger star shining far away above the familiar countenance of the moon. He began to write.

Chapter 3

Ellen had not spoken since she entered the building, but she was not seeking any kind of human encounter. She walked up and down the ancient stones, passing through shadows and shafts of muted light, lost in contemplation. The silence settled round her like a cloak and, glimpsed from a distance, her skirt reaching nearly to her ankles, she could have been some figure from a forgotten age, which glided before the flickering candles and paused in front of the high altar to bow its head. She loved the cathedral and, when she was not working, she often slipped in through the great wooden doors to spend an hour or two there on her own. She had started coming soon after the birth of Edward, carrying him in her arms like an offering, and she had returned in her spare moments ever since.

Today, she felt disturbed and unsettled. In her pocket lay the letter from her father. She had read it many times but could make no sense of it. She hoped fervently that his long hours of isolation were not affecting his mind, that he was not slipping into a world of fantasy. Perhaps she would go and visit him as he had requested – take a few days off work. It would be half term next week and it would be good for both her and Edward to get away; it would mean that she didn't have to leave him against his wishes, palm him off somewhere, ask favours she would find difficult to return. They were too much on their own, and had been since he was a baby. At nine, he was starting to have quite strong opinions, and she sometimes wondered how she would manage as he grew into his teens.

Her lunch hour was nearly over and she would have to make her way back to the office. She hated her job, felt it beneath her, knew that she should have changed direction as she had been planning when unexpectedly, shockingly, Edward was conceived, the result of an embarrassing and foolish night that would long since have been forgotten, but for the fair-haired and quietly determined child who had arrived and turned her life upside down.

Ellen walked over to one of her favourite parts of the cathedral. She would spend a few moments there before she returned to work. It was a quiet corner on the west side of the building, where a semi-circle of bricks had been placed upon the floor, touching the wall at either end and creating an enclosed space. Here, sand had been deposited and, in the sand, many candles burned, put there in grief or remembrance, in thankfulness or regret, or a thousand other reasons whispered in the hearts of those who came to pause a while, and leave behind their small flames of hope.

Taking a candle from the stand and dropping the coins into the box as she had done so many times before, Ellen paused whilst she reflected for whom or what to light it: Edward, her father, her mother, still so missed; Simon, way up north, living a life with his family that seemed so far removed from her own small world that sometimes she had to remind herself that they were brother and sister? Or should she light a candle for the world, battered and bruised, for its leaders who had lost their way, and were taking their peoples in directions which threatened destruction?

She lit the wick of her candle and watched the flame flicker, then she knelt to place it carefully in the sand. For a tense moment, she thought the tiny light would die before her eyes, but it shivered for a few seconds and then began to burn steadily.

"The world," murmured Ellen.

She stayed on her knees, lost in contemplation and, all around, the air was still, hushed as at midnight. At last, she rose to her feet. She was alone and the vast building felt deserted. She hesitated, suddenly afraid. She looked again at the candles and their lights of hope, then gasped. The sand was stirring, as if the wind blew across the yellow grains and ruffled their surface.

She hurried down the side aisle, fear catching at her throat. She must have been imagining things, but she felt as if the whole cathedral was shifting and that, at any moment, the stones would move, bringing the building crashing down upon her head.

She passed through the great doors and into the warm sunlight. All seemed unchanged. People hurried by, or paused to gaze up at the ancient steeple and turrets. A few turned to go into the cathedral. As she crossed the precinct, she glimpsed the headlines of a passerby's newspaper: 'Rumours of War'. Ellen shuddered. The papers were full of the likelihood of war, the TV channels relentless in reporting stories of aggression, the breakdown of talks, while social media spread fear and a growing despair. She turned to look at the magnificence of the cathedral, the beauty of its structure, marvelling at its endurance over hundreds of years. It had taken so long to build, such skill and perseverance to achieve its completion.

She was overcome for a moment with a deepening sense of foreboding. She must get away. She would tell Edward that they were leaving the city for a while, and going to visit his grandfather.

She glanced up once more to look at the sky, take comfort from its patterns and gentle movements of silver clouds. She felt the sunshine on her face, but it was not the blues and silvers which held her attention. She shook her head and stared more keenly, shading her eyes.

Far above the cathedral, solitary and enigmatic, hung a star. Ellen looked around to see if anyone else had noticed it, but people went about as usual, and seemed oblivious. She gazed once more into the far reaches above and, even as she knew that she was not mistaken, the star grew brighter.

Chapter 4

Simon and Catherine had moved up north soon after they were married. They had bought an old farmhouse on the edge of the village and, over the years, had made it into the home of their early dreams. Although Catherine's parents showed no particular concern at their departure, Simon found his own family full of deep regret. His father, in particular, grieved, although he never spoke of his feelings of loss. As a son, Simon understood and was sad at the pain he knew he was causing, yet he felt a strong calling to make another way of life, and the thought of the mountains and lakes, the space and uninhabited places, filled him with excitement.

They settled as if it had always been their home. On the surface, they appeared like any other ordinary family, bringing up Lachlan and Joquella, joining in the local community, going about their work with steady purpose. Underneath the calm rhythm of their days, however, beat another measure altogether, one that told them of the shortness of time, of the future slipping from their grasp even as they tried to picture its possibilities. In the village and surrounding district, the small nearby town where Simon was the local doctor and Catherine the district nurse, nothing really appeared to change, but in the world outside, in towns and cities, across the seas in other lands, an ever increasing brutality seemed to emerge. Although only forty, Simon sometimes felt twice that age for, whilst in his home and working life he was fulfilled and content, he felt an increasing constriction around his heart that somehow patterned the shrinking of the earth, even as it spun its journey.

He and Catherine talked for hours, long into the night when the children were asleep, or in their precious moments of freedom during the day, when they climbed up the hillside behind the house and sat at the top, gazing down upon the loch the other side. Simon knew that Catherine had a premonition she dare not express even to him and that, sometimes, those early dreams which had brought them to this beautiful place turned to nightmare. He did not ask, for he knew the time would come when she was ready to tell him.

On this early summer Saturday morning, no such disquieting thoughts disturbed him as he awoke, full of a sense of anticipation and excitement. He could hear the wind scurrying around the house as it often did, but the sun shone through the curtains, and he was alive with eagerness to go into the hills.

"Do you mind?"

Catherine was already pulling on her dressing gown, calling to the children to wake up, that the day was too beautiful to waste

"Of course not." She smiled. "I'll be back from my visits soon after lunch, but I'll be quite happy pottering about the house. Will you take the children?"

She knew that, devoted father as he was, he loved to roam the hills alone sometimes, and could find their chatter distracting.

"They can come if they're in the mood, and won't grumble at the climb."

Simon lifted his face and took a deep breath. The day smelled of hope and promise. Lachlan and Joquella bounded along at his side, swept up in the exhilaration of the day, and he felt a burst of tenderness for them, so vulnerable in their emerging maturity, so trusting in him as they laughed and scampered across the hillside.

"Perhaps we'll find the spring today," cried Joquella, and Lachlan slapped her playfully on the back.

"Silly girl, you know it's only a legend. You're as bad as the old men and women in the village who talk of hearing the sound of falling water at night."

Simon walked beside them lost in thought. He loved the ancient myths and legends of the area, and the story of the lost spring was his favourite. It had been the first fable he and Catherine had heard when they arrived in the village, told at one of the impromptu gatherings so popular with the villagers. He would never forget the atmosphere as the tale unfolded, how the goose pimples ran along his flesh. Old Callum had been the narrator. Now long since dead, he must have been at least ninety then, but he had not lost his piercing gaze nor the deep, compelling timbre of his voice.

"You're right, Lachlan, the story of the lost stream is a legend, but it has a truth at its heart."

"Tell us, Dad," urged Joquella.

Lachlan snorted, but Simon knew that the boy was intrigued.

"We'll have a rest in a while, then I'll tell you again, though I'm sure you two know every word yourselves."

As they climbed, the view of the surrounding mountains came into sharper focus, remnants of snow on their peaks, sun lighting the summits, the sky an azure backdrop for the rocky heights.

The path grew steeper as they walked, and Simon could see that the children were becoming tired.

"We'll stop here and have a drink and something to eat and, while you're resting, you can hear the old story once again."

Lachlan and Joquella whooped with pleasure, and followed their father to a grassy patch where they sank to the ground with relief. Handing out sandwiches and water, Simon realised that he felt a flutter of uneasiness, as though this telling of the legend had some unknown significance which he could not understand. He took a deep breath.

"Once upon a time."

The children laughed, and settled down to lie comfortably on the grass. There was no sound of birdsong, no running streams with their soothing melodies. It was as if the mountains themselves listened, and that the air was stilled and was waiting.

"For aeons of time, long before man walked upon these heights, it is believed that water sprang from the ground high above here, and then disappeared some way down the mountainside, before it reached the village. When the first settlers came, they were eager to find the source, and they followed the stream from where it disappeared from sight, climbing up the slopes beside the tumbling water. They came across it at last, springing from the ground close by the golden eagles' nesting place and they fell to their knees and drank.

"Imagine their astonishment when they found that the liquid appeared to have some strange power when they drank it, and that their exhaustion fell away from them like discarded skins. Even more curious, within hours of tasting the water, various ailments amongst those first explorers appeared to heal, and, when the other villagers heard of this, they started to go up the mountainside and drink the water, whilst those too weak to walk, were carried by the stronger ones.

"No-one ever attempted to take away any of the precious liquid. By mutual agreement, they decided that such an act would be a desecration and would bring the wrath of the natural world upon them. And so it was that, over countless decades, they made the pilgrimage to the source and drank there, and many were cured of sicknesses of both body and mind. And the wind always blew sweetly there, to cool their cheeks and calm their breath. So the people lived long years, and knew no lingering illness nor unquiet thoughts, and their world seemed set in harmony, and all was peace. They told no-one outside the village of their discovery and, for generation upon generation, it was a closely guarded secret.

"And then one day, long ago, everything changed. A stranger arrived in the village, dark and thin, with eyes that were sunken deep in his sockets, but eyes that glittered as if a fire smouldered within. He was sly and clever and, bit by bit, he turned the community upside down, talking of riches beyond their wildest imaginings and the foolishness of not using the water to make their fortunes. He divided the people so that, for the first time since the spring had been discovered, fathers quarrelled with sons, and husbands and wives turned against each other.

"When the first water was caught in casks and carried down the mountain to take away to some distant place, those who feared the consequences held their breath, gazing up to where the eagles flew beneath a darkening sky. Riches came at first, and those who grasped them laughed at those who would have nothing to do with the money. Then illness began to spread amongst the people like a creeping tide and those who were not ill grew discontented and sour. They still drank the water from the source, but there was no further healing. The liquid that had been captured and taken away stopped selling as it failed to bring the miraculous results promised.

"After a while, the villagers ceased their journeys to the source. The years passed with the seasons, and people no longer believed in the possibility of miracles. Then, one morning, three of the men who had witnessed the marvels of earlier days, decided to climb again to where the spring leapt into the air. They struggled up by the stream, which no longer tumbled but trickled down towards the valley. As they gained height, they became aware that the wind was not ruffling their hair, nor catching at their breath, although it had been sweeping through the village when they left, and was moaning now around the surrounding peaks, and they felt afraid. And, when they reached the top, the source of the stream no longer sprang from the earth; the grasses were dry and the land was cracked and crumbling, and when they looked back down the way they had come, the stream was no more, and the mountainside was bare."

Chapter 5

Simon jumped to his feet when he had finished speaking, and stood gazing up at the sky. For some reason he felt close to tears, and he did not want the children to notice, but Joquella followed him and slipped her hand into his. Lachlan stayed where he was, chewing a piece of grass, but he was silent too. They could hear birdsong now and, overhead, some gulls glided past them and disappeared. Simon smiled at his daughter.

"We'd better get going. We've still quite a climb."

The children responded eagerly, putting the water bottles into the rucksack, turning to look down the way they had ascended, then up to the path ahead and, in the bustle of the moment, Simon felt his heart lifting. In some way, for him, the legend symbolised the drying up of the very globe itself, and the shrinking of the human spirit, but he knew nothing was that simple. He looked around at the grandeur of the surroundings and thought of his own small footprints on their enduring paths.

"Come on Dad!"

The children were impatient to be gone, and Simon laughed as he followed them up the narrow route towards the heights. He watched as they climbed in front of him, chatting together as they often did. Joquella was slight for a twelve year-old, with an impish face and long, dark hair like her mother's. One day she would be beautiful, but for the moment she was protected by a deceptively immature manner and a complete unawareness of her own veiled loveliness. Lachlan took after him, and was altogether more sturdily built than his sister, with fair hair and humorous blue eyes. He would be tall in a year or two, but at the moment he came only to Simon's shoulder.

It was Joquella who first spotted the eagle, arching above them on the skyline like a magnificent but alien guardian of the upper reaches of the mountain. Its wings seemed to reflect the brilliance of the sun, stretched wide and golden against a sky of unbroken blue beyond the mountain crest. Even from their small vantage point, the power and concentration of the bird was palpable, and they drew breath at their own sudden sense of vulnerability.

Simon put his hand on the children's shoulders and drew them close to him. He had seen the eagles before, and had stood gazing at the pair as they soared above him but, today, it seemed as if this lone bird was watching them intently, and could see straight into their hearts. He wondered if it were one of the pair that inhabited this lonely mountain. To him, it was half angel, half demon, and into his vision sprang the piercing eyes, the beak that could tear flesh with ruthless efficiency, and the talons that would seize a prey without mercy and carry it away.

"Look," breathed Lachlan, "you would think it knew exactly what's in our minds."

Joquella nestled up against her father, and he felt the soft texture of her hair upon his arm.

"Let's keep climbing."

Simon did not reply to his son's remark, for he did not wish either to dismiss the words or give them credence, yet he knew that the boy was sensing his own apprehension and was suddenly afraid. So they walked on and, as they travelled, the path grew steeper and the vegetation more sparse. They were high above the tree line now and drawing closer to where the legend placed the vanished source of the stream. The peak seemed to bear down on their heads and, despite the sunshine, the air was much colder here. As they gained height, the way grew narrower and steeper, and stones dislodged under their feet, making them stumble. Tufts of grass grew spikily between the rocks, and boulders rose across the mountainside like custodians of stone. For Simon, the place had a haunting beauty, a quality of a paradise lost, a land locked in waiting whilst, all around, the vista fell away to unseen valleys, to distant peaks or, on very clear days, the sea. He thought he caught a glimmer of water now, but mist was gathering below and he could not be sure. The eagle still hovered above them, seeming to trace their steps as they drew nearer to their destination. They could see the last, sharp haul just ahead.

"Nearly there!" cried Lachlan and Joquella nodded with relief.

It took Simon a few moments to realise what he had been noticing over this last steep ascent; instead of hanging straight down to her shoulders, the girl's hair was moving slightly, as if some unseen hand ran its fingers through it and lifted the dark strands with an easy caress.

"The wind!"

The children turned back to gaze at him, startled, and Joquella brushed the hair away from her eyes and shook her head.

"But the wind never blows here."

"It's not that it never blows here, it's just that we've never heard it when we've been here."

"Well, I've never heard it before, even when it's been blowing in the valley," insisted Joquella, "but I can hear it now, and it's creepy."

They all listened to the noise: a murmuring as if the very mountain itself were speaking to them. Simon took the children's hands. He glanced up to the sky and saw that the eagle was gone.

"The wind is stirring, but that's not the sound of the

wind. That is water."

Catherine was home sooner than she expected and, for once, the house did not welcome her. It felt cold and empty despite the warmth outside, and she did not want to stay there alone. Although she knew she could not expect Simon and the children for some time, she kept on going out to gaze along the road in case three figures appeared in the distance and raised their arms in greeting.

The sun shone still and the day danced with promise, whilst the hill behind the house beckoned with its green paths and grassy summit. On impulse, Catherine changed into her walking boots and, five minutes later, she was climbing rapidly, humming her sense of relief out loud, shrugging off the unexpected spasm of loneliness that had clutched at her throat and driven her from the house. When she reached the summit she would see the loch on the other side, and she would rest for a while and let the view paint itself upon her senses.

She was not disappointed. The water shone beneath and, whichever direction she turned, the mountains spread around her, patches of snow still glittering on their peaks. She lay on the grass and closed her eyes. The sounds of nature floated round her: birdsong, the cry of a lamb in the distance, the murmur of the breeze as it cooled her cheeks.

Catherine did not know what prompted her to sit up. Perhaps it was the sudden chill as the sun slipped behind a cloud, or maybe it was the distant rumble of thunder she thought she heard. She looked around in apprehension, although she felt certain she was alone. Below, the loch was tranquil and she could see a small boat cutting across its surface. In the fields beyond its far shore, the sheep grazed lazily. She tried to force her gaze away, to start the descent back home, but she had no power to turn her head. She leapt to her feet, knowing what she would see. It was the vision of her dreams and her waking nightmare.

The loch was no longer peaceful and the boat had disappeared. The water was dark and angry, rain lashing its surface, and waves, churned to flecks of white riding the blackness underneath, raced to the shore. The fields beyond had lost their green pastures and were grey with mud, and no sheep wandered there searching for grazing.

Yet, the land was not empty. Trudging through the onslaught of the storm were thousands of people, struggling across ground which stained their feet and slowed their steps, some carrying infants too small to walk, or children too exhausted to go on, others supporting the old and infirm, untold and uncounted peoples searching for safety.

Catherine stood rooted, shaking, knowing that what she saw was the landscape of her mind, yet it was as vivid as if those suffering below were walking past her on the hillside. And she knew that all across the globe such people trekked, searching for sanctuary.

She saw the eagle then, carrying the tiny lamb in its talons. The creature was still alive, for she could see its struggling limbs and, in her wild fear, she thought she felt its breath against her face.

"No!"

At last she could move, and she started to run down the hillside. She ran until she was at the edge of the village and saw, coming towards her, Simon and the children. They stared in consternation as she approached, and Simon raced to catch her in his arms, hold her close against his chest. After a few moments, she raised her head and looked into her husband's eyes.

"I saw something from the hilltop," she whispered so that Lachlan and Joquella would not hear. "I've seen it before. Perhaps I've been watching the news too much, but it's more than that. We can't just wait here, Simon, when…"

She could say no more, as sobs racked her chest and tears fell unchecked. He struggled for words to bring her comfort, to tell her what had happened to him and the children so that she could find some hope.

Joquella came and put her arms around Catherine's waist.

"Don't cry, please don't. Wait till we tell you what we've seen today. You'll never believe it."

"Yes, and there was a single golden eagle flying way above us. You should have seen it, Mum." Lachlan longed to make his mother smile.

"And its wings shone like an angel's," cried Joquella, "although, to tell the truth, it was a bit scary."

Into Catherine's mind came the picture of the eagle with the lamb in its talons. It didn't have to be that way. She hugged Joquella close and kissed the top of her head.

"We'll go home and brew some tea, and you can tell me the whole story."

They walked back to the house chatting about simple, everyday things, the children linking arms as they used to do when they were younger, Simon with his arm around Catherine's shoulder; yet even as he smiled and joined in, another part of his mind was lost in contemplation of the terror he had seen in his wife's eyes, and the hope he knew shone in his own.

It was not until they were settled snugly in the kitchen drinking mugs of tea and munching home-made fruit cake, that Catherine remembered.

"There's a letter for you from your father. Sorry, I forgot."

He read slowly and, as he did so, his jaws ceased moving. When he had finished he handed the white paper, covered in the familiar black scrawl, to his wife. There was a hushed interlude as she absorbed the contents, then she looked at the expectant faces around her, the children's filled with curiosity, Simon's with concern.

"Somehow we shall have to go, all of us," she said, turning to Lachlan and Joquella. "Grandpa needs some help."

The children groaned at the thought of the long drive, and being stuck in their grandfather's small cottage, but Simon nodded and reached out to take Catherine's hand. They both knew that it would be difficult to organise, but they also sensed that the events of the day were connected with the call for help in the letter.

The phone rang and the children groaned again, holding their noses in mock disgust and making strangling noises in their throats. Simon laughed as he went to answer.

"It won't be a patient, so you can cease your caperings."

"Is Grandpa ill?" asked Joquella, and Catherine shook her head.

"It's not that."

"Then why?" began Lachlan, but his mother held up her hand. They could hear Simon's voice clearly.

"We're coming, Father, as soon as we've made arrangements. And we will help you if we can."

Chapter 6

Shayrath walked through the town in the early morning light. This was the best time of day, before the streets became crowded, and fumes choked the air. Even the shabbiness of the buildings seemed muted, the drab uniformity of the more modern ones diffused by the tentative sunrise, the older ones looking almost grand in the gentle light. There were a few people around, but not enough to break the quiet of the moment. In a while all that would change, and the noise and clamour would ricochet throughout the hours and beyond the coming of darkness.

A poster hung in a shop window. "War Rumours Again" it proclaimed in smudged, irregular letters. The people of this town knew war intimately. At twenty-five, Shayrath remembered only too well the noise from the bombs and the smell of fear as he trembled in whatever rough shelter they could find with his mother and younger brother. He remembered, too, the hatred for the enemy and the powerlessness of his people. His father had died in the fighting of the last war, as had both his uncles, the brothers of his mother. She had never been the same since, shrivelling up like an old piece of leather, her eyes sinking into her head as if retreating from her face, the fullness of her lips lost in the unrelenting determination not to smile.

There had been a kind of peace for some time now, but no sense of security. There seemed no hope amongst the people. The children still ran about the streets to play, and the market stalls were as busy as before the war, yet beneath the apparent normality surged an undercurrent of tension and suspense. There was no long term heed for tomorrow, because the day to day demanded all their energy and anyway, the past informed them that the future they had planned might not come.

Shayrath sighed. For a long time now he had felt out of tune with everyone he knew. His mother called him a dreamer, and despaired at his lack of ambition, his poorly paid job in the factory, the fact that he never showed any interest in women. Why, she asked him again and again, could he not be like his younger brother, Ethan, who was doing so well in the army.

Shayrath took no notice of her grumbling, still sharing with her the small, dark house that he had grown up in, looking after her when she would let him. For most of the time, he led a quiet and unexciting life very much on his own. He had always hated his home town and, in his spare time, spent many hours wandering around the countryside. At least, he had done so until these last months, when the urgency of his task had put him on another course.

He had been fascinated by the sky since he was very young. As a child, he would steal away in the daytime and find a secluded spot where he could lie on his back observing the clouds. When he was eight years old his grandfather gave him a dilapidated and ancient pair of binoculars, and on clear nights he gazed through these at the magnificent tapestry of the stars. He never grew tired of watching and, as he grew older, he taught himself as much as he could about astronomy, spending long hours, when he should have been asleep, reading old magazines discarded by the library, and checking the information by staring out of his bedroom window.

He had noticed the stranger star six months ago on a particularly translucent night, when the frost numbed his fingers and the moon lit up his breath. Since then he had traced its movements, and marvelled at its changing nature, for sometimes it seemed to grow in diameter and draw closer; at other times it was a distant smudge of light in the upper reaches of the sky. Each day he expected to hear that others had seen it too, and he listened eagerly to the news, to the chatter in the market place, but no mention of the mysterious planet was made, and he began to wonder if he was mistaken. Yet, whenever he scanned the night sky it was there and, once or twice, he thought he glimpsed it during daylight. For many weeks he was troubled, filled with apprehension and uncertainty, until an idea of what he must do slipped into his mind and, as the conviction grew, his sense of purpose drove him through the dreary days. Now, he longed for free time when he could work upon his task.

Shayrath glanced at the poster. How little the leaders understood, puffed up by power and ambition. They thought that death was for others, and had no concept of wider things. The country was a melting pot of faiths and no faith, but that brought no wisdom or comprehension to those who ruled them. Shayrath looked away from all the commotion, and found his understanding in the arching sky, and the never-ending script of stars and planets.

He started to run, desperate to leave the claustrophobic streets, and it was not until he reached the outskirts of the town that he slowed down. The air was cooler here, fresh and clear, and the river that wound along by the path had lost its city sludge. He did not look back, but he still felt the weight of what lay behind upon his heart: his mother, his people, the whole flimsy structure of the society in which he lived. The world.

He was crossing fields now and his feet disturbed the dry soil, creating small clouds of dust as he walked. He was the only human in all that landscape. The few trees he passed seemed to stir slightly as he walked by, and the empty land stretched as far as he could see, parched and uncultivated.

The sky hung over him like a silken shroud, wan sunlight touching his face, tentative in its early light. He hurried along a small track. Over to his left a deserted farmhouse stood amongst its forgotten smallholding and, some way behind it, reared a huge barn. Shayrath left the track and made his way across the fields to the abandoned buildings.

He and Ethan had stumbled across the farmhouse one day when they were still boys, and it had become for them an enthralling kingdom of mystery and excitement. Musty with the stale smell of forgotten human habitation, the place was filthy, glass on the floors, a broken-down chair and bed, a reminder of past dwellers, the passageways and staircase echoing with the tread of long dead feet. As children, they had not noticed the squalour, and they had made their plans there, away from adult eyes and the dullness of their everyday existence. They had spent hours inside, taking with them a bottle of water and some biscuits, matches and candles. Overcoming their fear was a challenge on each visit, but they would not be deterred by the shadows that stalked there, and they dreamt of future feats and wealth beyond imagining.

"What funny kids we must have been," mused Shayrath as he approached the buildings. He thought of his brother far away on the other side of the country, and had a sudden sharp pang of longing for that old, unquestioning companionship. He had never really made friends and, since Ethan's departure, he had been very much alone.

The barn rose before him. It was vast, more like an aircraft hangar than a barn; in fact it would dwarf even that, and Shayrath often puzzled over how such a building had come into existence and what its use had been. As children, they had avoided it after that first occasion, awed by the giant proportions of the building and the twilight gloom of the windowless interior. Great doors were pulled across one end, and it was obvious they had not been opened in years, for they were stuck fast and needed far greater strength than Shayrath's to move them. On one side of the wall, however, a small door yielded access, and it was through this that he now entered, glancing around before he did so to ensure that no eyes were watching. He was safe.

Once inside, he stood for a moment and waited for his heartbeat to slow down, his breath to subside. For reasons he did not understand, he always felt nervous when he entered, almost as nervous as that one and only time he had crept in with Ethan, expecting some unimaginable danger lurking inside. Now, he peered into the dusky space as he had done so many times over the past few months. It lay there alone, lifeless on the cold concrete. Shayrath pulled some matches from his pocket and lit the lamps he had taken in when he first started his work. The flames flickered, swelling into life like unbidden genii, casting shadows across the walls and resting on the object that lay upon the ground. He knelt down and ran his hand along the rough wood.

The tree filled the entire length of the barn and its branches spread out to touch the walls on either side. Once, it must have been the king within the forest, its toppling like the death of some revered ruler. It was obvious that it had lain in the barn for years, encased in this silent tomb, but how it could have been transported was a mystery. Some purpose long since forgotten had brought it there, dragged inside by hands now cleaned bare of all flesh. He still remembered the shock when he and Ethan had crept in all that time ago and seen it on the floor, immobile and lifeless, shocking in its immensity, its lost power. They had stood, spellbound, whispering their amazement and unease, and had left the building like guilty fugitives, never to return.

It was not until the appearance of the star that Shayrath thought again of the tree. Since that day with Ethan when they were boys, he had erased it from his mind but, when the star appeared, the memory of the fallen tree slipped into his head and took hold of his imagination. In all the upheaval of the world, he knew he was of no significance, disregarded and forgotten like so many others. Yet, as the beauty and enigma of the star drew him towards a different world, so he longed to create something of beauty himself, show those that lived in his frayed and neglected town that they could find a voice that needed no words.

The light from the lamps shone brightly now, and it could be seen that some of the branches had been cut off, and that someone had started to strip away the bark. It was a huge task, but he had no choice. He picked up the plane and began to work.

Chapter 7

Far away in the foothills of the great eastern mountains, Ethan was on manoeuvres with the army. They had been in the area for several days, and he loathed the place with a black and simmering disgust. The mountains rose like broken and decaying teeth, dry and stripped of vegetation, and the foothills were strewn with rocks and boulders, making progress difficult, whilst the stream beds were caked and dusty, arid channels in a bleak landscape.

He was tired, hungry and lost, for somehow he had become separated from his unit. He had no idea in which direction the base lay, nor how far away it was. The day was hot and sultry, and he could feel sweat upon his back and brow. They had been allowed no means of communication for the exercise, nor was there any landmark that could give him an idea of his location. The leader of their group had the instructions; if he didn't find the others he was stranded.

They had marched since early morning, before breaking up into smaller teams. The insistent beat of heavy boots had pounded in Ethan's head, until the terrain they crossed could have been valley or highway, so blinkered was his world. After they had separated into their groups, they had been ordered to rest for ten minutes before making the assault across the mountains, and Ethan had crashed to the ground and fallen straight into a deep sleep. On waking with a start, he found that there was no trace of his companions and, despite his increasingly urgent calls, the shrill blows upon his whistle, he remained alone.

"Whatever are they playing at?" he muttered to himself, trying to ignite some anger so that his rising unease would be subdued. Surely they couldn't have forgotten him or, even worse, left him behind deliberately? There must be some misunderstanding. He stood looking around, moving from one foot to the other, his tall, loose-limbed body tense, his fine and sensitive face taut with concern. He would give it five minutes and then he must make a move, although in which direction he had no idea. Nothing was familiar and, the more he stared around, the greater his bewilderment.

How had he got himself into this mess? Shayrath had warned him. Yet he understood why he was there: the stagnation of life at home, the poverty of his existence, the lack of any opportunity to improve his future in the small town. He had thought that the army would be a way out, an escape from a trap that seemed far worse than the regimented and demanding life he knew he would have to lead.

"You're such a gentle person, Ethan," Shayrath had said, "how will you cope with violence and death if you have to encounter them?"

Ethan smiled bitterly as he remembered his reply: "Anything is better than staying here! With luck, there won't be another war for a long time." How naive he had been; it did not take a war to begin the brutalization of a man.

As he stood wondering what to do, trying to quell the rising panic, the fear of being lost in this wilderness, or being found and punished for getting separated from his unit, a sudden gentle breeze touched his face and cooled his heated brow. He closed his eyes for a few moments, savouring the comforting touch. He would wait a little longer and hope his comrades returned to find him.

He lost all sense of time as he stood there but, when he looked around again, he was shaken out of his lethargy. What was happening? Perhaps the heat was affecting him and he was hallucinating; he felt dehydrated and tired, so he must be creating pictures in his mind. He tried to steady his breathing, pull himself together, remember his training. Then he looked around again.

Mountain peaks still soared above him, but they were not the scarred summits he had seen earlier. These mountains rose snow-capped against a steel-blue sky and, at his feet, the grasses shone with summer flowers. He could hear running water in the distance, and sense the freezing blast from the glaciers that hung in sheets of ice high above his head. Forgetting his predicament, drawn by a longing which tugged his heart with beating insistence, he turned his face towards the nearest foothills and began to climb. For the moment he had forgotten his lost companions, the trouble he would encounter if he ever returned to base. His eyes were fixed on the path ahead, on the light that clothed the fell side, and the streams that tumbled towards the valley. The mountains did not stir but, above, the sky seemed to bound with the breeze, and the few white clouds dipped and swayed. The air was filled with a multitude of murmurings: the streams and quiet wind, the unseen creatures of the uplands, and the birds that flew in distant patterns overhead.

Ethan moved as if kind and sensitive fingers had slipped between his own to take him like a child up towards the summit. He walked for some time, through cooling copses and across grassy slopes, following the track that must finally lead to the distant glacier and the peaks beyond. As he climbed, the air seemed to grow quieter, the sounds falling away behind him. He did not feel afraid, but he was filled with a strange anticipation so that he kept on looking around as though expecting to meet someone, to hear the rustle of footsteps which could not be explained.

As he gained height he saw a ridge in the distance, obscuring what lay above. He hurried forward, eager to discover what was hidden from sight, and hauled himself up. At the top, he paused for breath and looked around, unprepared for what he saw.

A little way in the distance lay a large wood. Perplexed, Ethan shook his head: surely at such a height, this was a strange discovery? The trees looked as if they had been transplanted from an ancient forest, their trunks thick and sturdy, their branches covered in leaves. He wanted to turn around and make his way back down the mountain, but some unseen force seemed to draw him forward and, a few moments later, he found himself entering the quiet twilight of another world. The trees gathered round him like sentinels as he stumbled to find a path, straining to see in the half light, and he longed to reach the far side and come out into the open.

The clearing came as a complete surprise, and he hesitated for a few moments, his heart pounding. All was completely still. He stepped from the soft, brown earth onto a carpet of grass, a perfect open circle amongst the trees, with the light pouring through in blinding shafts so that at first he could see nothing but its brilliance. How long it was before he realised he was not alone he never knew; he stood rubbing his eyes, waiting for them to adjust to the sudden glare, feeling the heat beating on his brow. When he could open his eyes fully, he thought at first that the vision he encountered was another wild hallucination, and he turned away for a few moments, then looked again.

The lamb appeared so relaxed and unconcerned it could have been in a farmer's field, nestled against the wool of its mother in the warm sunshine. It seemed hardly more than a day old, its coat gleaming white, its spindling legs stretched out, its small nose and eyes black against the creamy face. But it did not lie beside its mother, nor were there any signs of its kith or kin.

"My God!" whispered Ethan. He felt the hairs at the back

of his neck tingling, and the sweat running down his back. He wanted to run, but his legs were leaden, rooting him to the ground. He wanted to call out loud for help, but he knew that he was quite alone, lost in a world beyond his understanding.

The smoky grey fur of the wolf glistened in the sunshine. The long, muscular legs were tawny against the grass and the animal's paws were still. Even though it was lying down, Ethan felt the fierce strength of its body. The mouth was closed around the sharp teeth, so that the face looked almost gentle as it rested its head on the ground.

"My God," whispered Ethan again, and the whole mountainside seemed to echo with the words. "Where's the rest of the pack?" he thought, shaking with fear. Why had he climbed the mountain? What was happening to him? He expected at any moment to hear a dreadful howling, to be surrounded, defenceless. He tried to tell himself that such thoughts were nurtured on fairy tales, yet he could not help thinking of those savage teeth and the tearing of flesh. He waited for the creature to attack him, for the fangs to sink into his skin, and knew that he did not have the strength to resist.

Nothing happened. There was no noise but the call of birds out of sight above the trees, and a wind which stirred even as he listened for more sinister sounds. The animal lay there without moving, the tiny lamb encircled by the great paws, its head resting against the fur of the wolf as if the softest pillow lulled it to rest. The wolf gazed at Ethan without blinking, its green eyes pools of unfathomable desire.

"Oh help me," whispered Ethan, and at last his legs obeyed his will and he started to back away, shielding his eyes with his hand. Leaving the circle of light, he became a slight shadow amongst the ancient trees. He touched the trunks as he fled, grazing his palms on the bark, but he did not notice.

When at last he came out onto the open mountainside, he started to run, stumbling and catapulting himself down the way he had climbed up and, as he ran, he felt as if the sky itself were chasing him, to gather him into its arms and make him its own.

Chapter 8

Ethan could see the town in the distance. Smoke from factory chimneys rose in snakes of grey, and tower blocks were silhouetted against the sky in blank uniformity. He did not know where he was but, however ugly, the place held out hope of rest, food and shelter.

He had left as soon as he could, when the grim interview was over and he had listened to the warning words about nondisclosure, signed the confidentiality document. The senior officers had looked at him in disdain.

"Obviously, you are not fit to serve as a soldier. You have broken the fundamental code – never to leave your comrades. They waited on the spot where you deserted them for many hours. You are mentally unstable."

Ethan had felt their contempt and anger and something deeper, hidden beneath the unreflecting eyes.

He had handed in his uniform and dressed again in his civilian clothes. Glancing in the mirror as he changed, he saw a tall young man, dark hair cut short emphasizing high cheek bones, brown eyes, a thin and slightly pointed nose. In contrast, his lips were full and generous but, already, faint lines were etched at the corner of his mouth. He looked older than his twenty two years. He had not seen Shayrath or his mother for over twelve months; they would be shocked at his appearance.

The town was drawing closer. The road had been almost deserted, but now the occasional car passed, and ahead he could see the first sprawl of houses, poor looking dwellings, squat beneath the shadow of the factories behind. He had been walking for days with little rest or food, and exhaustion threatened to overwhelm him. He stumbled, his eyes blurring and, at that moment, a dog leapt up at him, barking menacingly. He whimpered like a child, trying to fend off the animal with his arms and feet, afraid that if he fell down he would be at the creature's mercy. The world spun in circles of red and black, and he pitched forward into the abyss and knew no more.

Once upon a time the caravan must have been brightly painted in cheerful colours, a flamboyant expression of an unshackled and independent way of living. Now the paint had faded, exposing here and there patches of bare wood yet, despite its faded splendour, it still hinted at the mystery and excitement of another way of life.

The horse grazing beside the van was an old piebald which, like its shafted chariot, had seen better days. The fire smoked lazily, and the three men grouped around it were not speaking, but sat staring into the flames.

"Feeling better?"

Ethan started. No-one had as much as glanced in his direction, where he lay on the grass wrapped in a rug like a swaddled infant.

"Thank you, I think I am." He wasn't sure. His whole body ached and his head felt twice its normal size. "What happened? Where am I?"

They were all looking at him now, inscrutable, unhurried, assessing. Two of the men were swarthy, dark skinned from the open-air life. The third was slighter, his complexion and hair fairer.

"We found you lying on the side of the road. A wild dog was taking an unhealthy interest in you. They roam around here in packs. But you have not been hurt."

The slight man was speaking, his voice surprisingly deep. Ethan guessed he was in his late forties; the other two looked older, perhaps in their middle sixties, but he could not be sure. The outdoor life must take its toll upon the skin.

"You saved my life!"

There was a long silence, broken only by the crackle of the fire and birds singing of approaching dusk.

"Hardly; now come and sit with us and share our food," said one of the older men, "you have great need of some sustenance."

Ethan disentangled himself from the blanket and went over to join them. He felt weak and emotional. He did not ask their names, nor they his. For some reason, it didn't seem appropriate to introduce himself, to ask about their identity. They were obviously gypsies, travellers across a landscape unknown to him, and he puzzled that they were alone; where were the rest of their people, the other men, the wives and children, the clutter and vibrancy of a nomadic life?

The youngest man was ladling a broth of roughly chopped vegetables and herbs into what looked like clay bowls. The aroma was intoxicating. Ethan could not remember when he had last eaten properly, and he was famished. There appeared to be no implements with which to eat, and he was about to dip the bread he had been given into the dish, when he realised that the others sat motionless with the bowls of food in their hands. Then the darker of the two older men, eyes slate grey like the rocks high up the mountainside, spoke rapidly in a language Ethan did not understand, but he knew they were giving thanks, and shame swept over him that he had not paused for even the briefest moment to be thankful.

Darkness fell as they ate. They passed more bread to one another, dipping the pieces into their bowls to scoop up the savoury mixture, and the youngest gypsy poured rich red wine from a flagon into cracked and stout goblets, and handed them round their small circle. The fire crackled, the flames licking the night with orange tongues. No-one spoke.

The meal finished, Ethan longed to lie down again and sleep, but he did not like to move. They sat round the fire, staring at it as if it contained the key to all mysteries. When he first noticed the metamorphosis, he thought he must be dropping off to sleep, and that his feverish mind was creating nightmare images. The flames were changing shape, growing as he watched, and he found himself shrinking backwards, holding his hands in front of his eyes for protection, stumbling to his feet before he fell to his knees. He turned in terror to his companions.

"It's going to crash!"

They did not stir, nor show any sign of agitation. The star hung above, lighting the grasses, hovering over their heads in a blazing orange and gold immensity.

The hands lifting him to his feet were gentle, the voices like the murmuring of a mother's song.

"Open your eyes," they said, and Ethan saw the fire burning brightly, with the stools set around it and the old, blackened, pot steaming quietly amongst the flames. The star hung high in the sky, the brightest in all the firmament.

"Who are you? Why do you travel alone?"

"We saw you running down the mountain, and have been waiting for you to arrive."

Ethan turned to the youngest man in bewilderment.

"Were you on the mountain? Did you see?"

"Only you can fully comprehend what you saw. Only you can respond."

"I don't understand." Ethan could have wept with frustration.

They drew him back to the fire, and sat him on a stool, and gave him a goblet of warm, comforting liquid. His head spun, and he thought that any moment he would fall off the seat unconscious.

"Rest again," they said when he had drunk, and led him to the place where he had been before, and wrapped the old blanket around him. Slowly, Ethan felt sleep overcoming him. The murmuring of the men's voices was a strange lullaby and, in his descent into oblivion, he thought he saw more people gathering around the fire. The star lay behind his closed eyes, blazing white and swept with golden flames and, in the flames, an ancient script contrasted its dark letters across the moving light.

"What does it mean?" whispered Ethan as he closed his eyes.

He felt a hand on his brow.

"We are awake and will keep watch tonight," said the gypsy, "but from tomorrow you must be alert at all times yourself. You must be ready when the time comes."

Ethan was too tired to ask for what he must remain watchful. He sank into a deep sleep, and the men gazed at him for a while, then turned away to leave him resting.

Chapter 9

Ethan awoke stiff and cold, the dew of morning dampening his blanket. In an instant he remembered the events of the previous evening, and he called out hello before he stirred, opening his eyes to greet his companions.

The gypsies were nowhere to be seen. The caravan and old, piebald horse had vanished and the fire, charred and blackened, lay dead in its ashes. He struggled to his feet, pulling the blanket with him, calling aloud as he did so, searching in vain for the three men. He felt abandoned and afraid. He ran to the road and gazed up and down, half expecting to see the wagon in the distance, its faded splendour still colourful against the drab monotony of the surroundings, but the way was empty. He glanced up at the sky; the star was nowhere to be seen, but the moon still hung in pale and misty silver far above him.

"They've gone."

The man sitting on a nearby tree trunk was smiling but, despite this, Ethan took an involuntary step backwards. The cold clung to his body and he was shivering.

"Gone?"

"Typical gypsies, well rid of them."

"Did you see which way they went?" Ethan could not stop himself from asking the question, although he did not wish to show this stranger his growing concern.

"No idea. What is it to you?"

The eyes were sunken deep into the man's sockets but, from their depths, Ethan glimpsed a flash, as if they glittered briefly. He shrugged his shoulders, tried to appear nonchalant.

"Nothing. Just wondered."

The stranger smiled again, thin lips parting to show small, pebble teeth. He was tall, with a head disconcertingly small for his body. The black hair was sleeked back as if for some old photograph, the cheeks white and pulled tautly across his face. He was dressed in a dark suit with a red shirt and tie; it seemed a strange outfit for someone sitting on a tree trunk outside town in the early hours of morning.

Ethan did not reply. He wished the man would go, for there was something unsettling about his presence. To make matters more awkward, he realised that he was still clutching the blanket and had not shaved or washed for several days. He must look like a vagabond in his muddy and crumpled clothes.

"Are you coming to the demonstration?"

"Demonstration?" Ethan parried the question, knowing he would go nowhere with this unwelcome and intrusive stranger.

"There's only one demonstration today. Ah well, if you're not interested, I'll be going," and he nodded knowingly, his hidden eyes seeming to challenge Ethan to curiosity.

The town was much larger than he had expected, and it looked as though the whole population had turned out for the demonstration. Men and women of every generation, babes in arms and toddlers, older children, crowded onto the streets, and Ethan found himself swept along amongst a tide of humanity that moved as one body with a single purpose. After a while the streets opened into a large square where thousands were massing, pouring in from every direction, chanting and carrying placards: Give Us Peace Not War, Save Our Children, No, Not Again. Ethan turned to the old woman standing beside him.

"What war is this?"

She turned to look at him, her face lined with suffering

and endurance.

"You don't know?"

Ethan shook his head and was about to ask another question, when a shot rang out and a mounted policeman nearby fell from his horse and disappeared from sight amongst the trampling feet. The crowd stirred uneasily and, even as he looked around, Ethan saw another policeman fall to the ground.

"Whatever…?" he gasped.

As if his head were attached to a string pulled by a master puppeteer, his eyes were drawn to a towering monument in the middle of the square. Ethan recognised him with chilling certainty. The man stood on the plinth, dark against the pale marble, the gun held steady in his hand.

"Look!" he shrieked, but no-one took any notice. As the third shot exploded into the air, the crowd bucked and started to stampede while, from every direction, gunfire shattered the morning sky.

He was running and running, blindly, gasping in sobbing breaths of terror. He could see no end to the road ahead, nor to the crowds of fleeing people.

"Where's the enemy?" he cried to those who ran beside him. "Isn't there any transport, something to help us escape?"

"There's no help. Run!"

"Where are we going?" he cried, but no-one could answer him on that flight from death although, all around, they were dying as they ignored his question.

The noise had intensified: the shouting, the blast of gunfire and explosions. On and on the people ran down the grey, pitted road, not stopping when someone fell, not pausing when the explosions shook the ground under their feet, or when the acrid air made them gasp for breath. Ethan felt his chest constricting and knew that he could not keep going much longer.

"It's no use fleeing!" he cried. "We can't escape. We're probably running straight into a trap!"

No-one seemed to hear him. He staggered to the side of the road and pressed himself against one of the concrete posts that separated it from the dilapidated buildings beyond. He looked around, trying to remember his training, but it was of no use. Although the people were being attacked, he could see no sign of the aggressors. He tried not to think about the children, the desperate mothers, the old woman who had fallen by his side. Remorse and pity swept over him, yet how could he have helped them?

The sudden roar of vehicles caught him unaware and he crouched against the post, trying to make himself invisible. People were scattering in all directions as they saw the trucks approaching: heavily armoured, racing without regard for those who could not get out of the way in time. Ethan was bewildered. He had not realised that he was so close to any army post, and how could they have responded so quickly unless they had been expecting trouble. The demonstration had seemed peaceful and the police had been out in force. What was going on? Into his mind flashed the memory of the officers the day he had been discharged, their uneasiness, their dimmed expressions masking something akin to fear.

"And that man," he thought.

How long he crouched there he did not know but, when he opened his eyes, the trucks had vanished and all was quiet. The crowds had disappeared as if they had never been, and no figures lay on the ground. He thought he heard shouting in the far distance, but he could not be sure. Ethan put his hand to his face and felt moisture, though he did not know why he was crying: for the people he had seen falling to the ground, tumbling into death like rag dolls; for himself, lost and alone, deserter and deserted; for the vision he had seen on the mountainside and had fled, even as he was fleeing now?

He stood up, wondering what to do. Somehow he must reach home and talk to Shayrath. He started to walk away from the town and, as he trudged along, the star slipped unnoticed into the high reaches of the sky, and shone above him.

Chapter 10

Four days later, Ethan jumped off the lorry on the outskirts of his home town. He looked around and felt his heart sinking. Nothing seemed to have changed.

He had walked for three days after escaping the carnage, avoiding any villages or places that showed signs of habitation, sleeping in ditches, cold and miserable, drinking from the occasional stream, without food or shelter of any kind. On the third day, he had been limping along some unknown road when he heard a vehicle coming up behind. The lorry driver had stopped. "Where're you going?"

Ethan told him with no sense of hope. The likelihood of the man heading for some obscure town away from any main conurbation wasn't even worth thinking about.

"Hop in. You're in luck."

Ethan could have wept with relief.

The warmth of the cab after his nights outside was luxury. He sat in the lorry for hours as they travelled across the country, letting the chatter of the driver drift over his head, sleeping in the back of the lorry, snacking at wayside cafes. The driver seemed oblivious to any news of demonstrations, nor did he show any curiosity about his passenger, but grumbled cheerfully about the state of the country and the bad behaviour of his children. Ethan found it comforting.

Now he had reached his destination, the events of the past days rushed in on him, and he felt cold with foreboding. Perhaps the army had only let him go in order to get rid of him, with no need for tiresome explanations. His dismissal had been too easy. He headed towards the centre of the town, to the drab street where he had grown up, and the house in which his mother and Shayrath still lived. He wondered what sort of reception he'd receive; his mother did not like the unexpected.

The poverty of the place struck him afresh, and the rush and mess of everyday life attacked his senses with their sights and smells, their noise and clamour. There were posters stuck in shop windows and tied to lampposts saying War Rumours, Where Are The Shelters? but he could see no reference to the scenes he had witnessed just a few days before. He met no-one he knew as he walked and, after a while, he reached the shadows of his own street. He stood for a few moments gazing around; then, with some trepidation, he went and knocked on the brown and dingy door of home.

His mother's face had sunk even further, her eyes and mouth retreating into her skull. The anger and bitterness were still there, and her refusal to see the smallest glimmer of hope had long since stripped her features of any softness. Ethan was shocked. He took a step towards her and held out his arms, but she cried out and started to back into the doorway; she had not recognised him.

"Mother!" He was hungry to be acknowledged, to be held even for a moment, and remember distant times that had once had offered reassurance. "It's Ethan!"

"Ethan?" She peered at him in disbelief and horror. "Whatever have you done to yourself? What are you doing here? Are you on leave? You should've warned me."

He hesitated. He hadn't considered what explanation he would give to his mother. He decided to tell the truth.

"I've left the army. I'm here while…" but his stammered words were lost in the vehemence of her rage.

"Left the army! Why? Have you gone mad! Am I forced to put up with two no-good sons!" She started to sob.

"Please Mother, it'll be okay. Shayrath and I'll take care of you. I'll get work."

"Shayrath! He's never here. Gone for hours, goodness

knows where."

Ethan tried to remain calm. She must have had a great shock at his appearance. He knew he looked terrible, with filthy clothes and hair, his face haggard. He would leave her to get used to the idea of his homecoming.

"I'll go off for a couple of hours and come back. I've startled you."

He was about to turn away when she stepped forward suddenly and laid her hand on his arm.

"You look dreadful. You can't go off in that condition. You'd better come in and have a shower and something to eat. Your clothes are in the wardrobe."

He followed her into the house without speaking, the confining atmosphere closing round him, the twilight hall chilly despite the warmth outside.

"Thanks Mother."

Ethan headed away from the town with relief. He had decided to go back to the old haunt where he and Shayrath had spent so many happy hours together as boys. He needed space to think. By the time he returned home, Shayrath might be there.

Although he was pleased to be away from the busy streets, he was appalled by the appearance of the land. The river that wound along by the path had lost its city sludge, but it appeared shrunk as though the water was draining out of it and, as he walked across the fields he saw that the ground was parched and bare, with no sign of any attempt at cultivation. The few trees had lost their foliage, although the grey branches seemed to stir slightly as he walked past. There must have been another drought, though he had heard nothing about it.

The barn rose ahead of him, as vast as in his memory,

not shrunk by older eyes, and he remembered with a shiver the day he and Shayrath had first crept in there and found the tree. He would not go near it today; it was the house he had come to see. He approached cautiously; it looked more derelict than ever and he hesitated, afraid suddenly of what he might discover.

"Idiot" he muttered and pushed open the front door. An odour of decay and neglect assailed him as he stepped inside, and the beating of wings suggested that he had disturbed birds unused to human intrusion.

"Shayrath?"

He didn't know why he called out, except that longing to see his brother swept over him. Why, they hadn't returned since they were young teenagers and it was absurd to think that Shayrath would be here now. He looked around, making out shapes in the gloom, seeing through half open doors the unchanged desolation of the years. At the top of the broken staircase he saw a large hole in the roof and debris on the floor beneath. What had induced them to spend so many hours here as boys? How impoverished and lonely they must have been. There was nothing for him here now, and it was with a great sense of relief that he pulled the door behind him and felt fresh air on his face. He would go back home, see if Shayrath had returned.

He was about to leave, weary all of a sudden, deflated and miserable, when he glanced upwards. He started in surprise as fear rushed over him. It hung over the barn, a pale reflection from a distant world, almost lost in the surrounding brightness, motionless and half-hidden. As his heart steadied, Ethan looked more closely, searching for the flames he had seen on its surface, or any sign that it might leave its own constellation and come towards him. It hung there still, pale and enigmatic, and beneath it the barn's sombre bulk stood dark and blind before him. Against every instinct that cautioned him not to, Ethan crossed the concrete and opened the small door that he remembered from all those years ago.

Huge shadows on the wall swayed in the lamplight. There was no sound or movement. The great tree lay entombed as he had last seen it, filling the space with its ruined presence. Nothing stirred, but kneeling by the tree was a figure which, to Ethan's bewildered mind, looked as though it grieved by the graveside of a lost loved one. It could be no-one else.

"Shayrath!"

"Ethan! Ethan, is that really you!"

Leaping to his feet, Shayrath half ran, half stumbled into the arms of his brother. The two men sobbed as they clung to each other, and a long time passed before either spoke. It was Shayrath who drew back and gazed with concern at his brother.

"What's happened Ethan? What are you doing here; I didn't think you had any leave?"

"I don't, I'm not on leave. I've left the army. I'll explain later. I'd rather not talk about that now; I just want to hear about you."

"Just tell me that you're well." Shayrath looked at his brother with increasing concern. "You look so thin and strained."

"I'm not ill." The brothers were standing apart now, observing each with troubled eyes, both seeing lines of strain that had not been evident a year ago. "What are you doing here, Shayrath? We always kept away from this place after that day."

"You'll think I've gone mad. Sometimes I think so too. It's everything: the talk of another war, always war, and the drought, nothing being done, rumours of the seas rising, forests destroyed. I felt so helpless. Then I got this sudden conviction, as if I were being told to do something. I just thought maybe…" Shayrath shrugged his shoulders. "When

I try to put it into words, I don't understand anything."

"But the tree? We were scared. Something must've brought you back."

"I think it was the star. It was after I first saw the star that the idea just popped into my head. I know it sounds crazy, but once that happened, I felt I didn't have a choice."

"Star!"

"Yes, the star that appeared one day way up in the sky, like a stranger from another realm. Funny thing is, no-one but me seems to have noticed."

Ethan shook his head slowly.

"A star? I think I've seen it too."

"You've seen it too!"

"What can it mean, Shayrath?"

"I don't know, but we must be ready when the time comes."

Ethan glanced around with apprehension, as if the shadows cupped their ears and shifted silently.

"Have you been talking to the gypsies? How could they have travelled such a long way?"

"Gypsies, what are you talking about!"

"The gypsies I met, that's what they said. We must be ready. Ready for what?"

"I don't know. All I know is that I have to do this."

For the first time, Ethan smiled.

"Well, I'm home and can help you, whatever that means." He looked at the tree for a few moments, then turned to his brother in bewilderment. "But what is it you're trying to do?"

"I'll try to explain, but it doesn't make sense, even to me, and it's not connected to anything I've ever done before."

The two brothers stood together gazing at the tree. Although they knew the wood was dead, the huge skeleton seemed enfolded in a history beyond comprehension, and emitted an aura of lost power, a presence that filled the vast spaces and silent air.

"Tell me what I must do."

Shayrath took his brother's arm and pointed to the trunk of the tree.

"You can start there."

Ethan took a step forward, then hesitated.

"It sounds crazy, but I feel afraid suddenly, as if I'll be wounding it in some way."

Shayrath shook his head.

"I think that happened a long time ago."

Ethan knelt down and ran his hand along the bark.

"I've so much to tell you too," he murmured. "Nothing seems to make sense to me either, except that I'm home with you."

Shayrath handed his brother a plane.

"We can talk later. For now, let's just work together."

Abiding With Silence

The pattern of the universe was changing. The moons were darkening and, far out beyond the reaches, the planets shifted imperceptibly and came closer. Amongst all the stirring constellations, the great star stood alone. It had appeared like a mysterious stranger from another realm one night and, as darkness came each day, it seemed to watch over them as they walked to Evening Worship. At times, tongues of flame burned about its surface, and the Counsellors gazed at the ancient script with awe.

The people carried on the daily pattern of their lives but, at times of worship, there was an intensity in the atmosphere that had not been there before. One day, Hedron stood in front of the table, the table which had been sculpted from wood of the forest long ago, the carvings on the surface depicting the life of the people, the flow of the seasons, and held out his arms.

"We know that we must wait. Now is the time to keep silence and be patient. We cannot know until everything is made clear to us."

In the fields and at the food gathering, at meal times and work places, they shared the rhythm of their lives without questioning. And as dusk came and the sky revealed its tapestry of stars, they watched in wonder as they had always done.

Hedron and Nathan were taking their usual evening stroll to the very edge of the dwellings, from where they could see the path which led the way to the plain and the Tree.

*"I feel I am standing on the very edge of our world,"
said Nathan, "and that if I take a few steps forward I will*

tumble into the medley of stars and hear the whispers of their language."

Hedron smiled at the younger man.

"You are sensing the movement all around."

"The flames, which sometimes seem to write their script upon that star. Are we called to understand it?"

Hedron shook his head.

"That star comes from skies hidden from us. We cannot imagine its history or its journey through unfathomable constellations. It has travelled from farther away than even the most distant galaxy, such distances that we cannot envisage its beginning; I feel it has appeared for a purpose and, as it draws closer, so does the final consummation."

"You once said that, beyond our knowledge, events unfold that clash and cleave, destroy and build, bring a great darkness and a saving light. You sensed there would be a calling in and a final consolation."

"I believe that still and, in some way, the stranger star is its harbinger."

"Do my parents see it?" murmured Nathan.

There was a long pause whilst the two men gazed at the sky, watching the star as it expanded with light and seemed to draw closer.

"Galen and Anna? I understand your longing. It is not for yourself. I still believe that we are part of an incomprehensible mystery where the very patterns of creation are stirring. Somewhere, Galen and Anna are a part of that pattern. I can say no more than that."

"And the Tree?" Nathan's voice trembled as he asked the question.

"Still abiding in all its unchanged glory."

Without further words, the two men turned to begin their walk back to the Centre of Worship.

"Our people are so faithful," said Nathan. "They never

ask."

Into both their minds slipped an image of the fine face, the tumbling curls, blonde almost to whiteness.

"You are very like your father," said Hedron, "both in appearance and grace. But his one flaw, to seek knowledge which should never be sought, you do not have."

They walked on in silence. Nothing more could be said and, as they approached the Centre of Worship, the star shone down upon their heads and gave them comfort.

Chapter 11

In the village shop, the talk was all about the possibility of war. An animated discussion was taking place on the subject of good and evil, but no-one could agree where evil emanated from nor who or what was good.

"Look," cried a young man Toran recognised as a farm worker from one of the local farms, and who obviously thought he numbered amongst the good, "we can't just sit back and let the forces of evil overrun us can we!"

"Who are they?" asked a quietly-spoken, elderly lady waiting by the checkout with her meagre basket. The young man ignored her.

"You've heard what the government says. If we don't attack first, they'll destroy us."

"Quite." The man who spoke was middle-aged and authoritative. "It's the only way."

"No war is worth the sacrifice. In the end it's the victory of our worst instincts over our potential for good." The shopkeeper spoke with passion, the strength of his feelings overcoming any caution he might have at the possibility of offending some of his customers.

"Nonsense!" The man looked indignant. "There've always been wars. Sometimes they're necessary."

"War is death," said the elderly lady, "a dying child, the screams of a wounded soldier from whichever side; these things are defeat and desecration."

Toran stood in the shop doorway, the warmth of the morning sun on his back, his voice startling them because no-one had noticed his presence.

"The evil is our refusal to see and acknowledge the humanity of others. It spreads across our world like poison,

67

but we could overcome it."

The middle-aged man snorted. "Such talk is surrender. I've no patience with it."

"Let's change the subject," said the shopkeeper. "No-one in power will take the slightest notice of what we say."

Toran shrugged his shoulders. He did not know why he had spoken; the fullness of time would sweep away all such conversations like spray blown across the waves. Without speaking again, he bought the few supplies he needed, and then, nodding farewell to the shopkeeper, he stepped with relief into the fresh air outside.

It was another glorious day. Toran shook his head, trying to rid his mind of disturbing thoughts, struggling not to see in the white and innocent clouds, future devastation. As always, when he felt uncertain or afraid, he headed for the church, going through the graveyard until he reached his favourite bench, up against the old stone wall, and there he sat until his heartbeat steadied and he began to relax and draw comfort from the peace.

The church rose before him in perfect contours, the spire etched against the sky. For Toran, the building was an old friend, loved and admired, cherished and never taken for granted. He valued coming here more than ever now, for Jane was buried close to where he rested and, since she died, he had often sat on this bench and told her of his heartache and his fears. The view from here had been her favourite and she had often come to sit where he was now, gazing out to sea.

He could not be long. He put the few supplies from the shop into his rucksack: a sandwich for himself, food for Solace, a baby's bottle, some milk. He had brought some scissors with him so that he could enlarge the hole in the teat, in the hope that the lamb would take a little nourishment. He frowned as he did so, for he was struggling to remember the route to the arena on the cliff, and the length of the walk. Now he thought back upon the previous day, he had no clear recollection of time or journey once he had met Solace. How could he retrace his steps without becoming lost? Simon, Catherine and the children were arriving early that evening; he would have to be home in time to welcome them.

Toran knew he must make a move, yet he did not stir. The sun shone down upon him, and he felt himself relaxing further, his eyelids closing against his will. The birdsong lulled him into dreaming, whilst the breeze lifted his hair and caressed his skin. The hands of the church clock shifted as he dozed, moving across its broad face to catch the passing minutes. Shadows played along the churchyard walls and the graves lay undisturbed in the morning light, cradling their dead in the rich earth.

It was the click of the gate that woke him. Startled, he rubbed his eyes, surprised that anyone should be approaching from the fields rather than along the main pathway. Two men were walking towards him, both sturdy and dark-haired, dressed as if they worked in the open, their faces tanned and weather-beaten. They carried roughly carved sticks and each had a much worn rucksack slung across his shoulders.

The men greeted him with friendly smiles as they drew nearer, and Toran found himself responding with pleasure, taking the outstretched hands and introducing himself. Strong and young, perhaps in their middle-thirties, they could have been his sons.

"I'm David and this is my brother Philip," said the slightly taller man. Toran did not recognise the man's accent; he certainly did not come from these parts, but there was something engaging about his manner, an openness that invited trust. Both brothers seemed very relaxed, in no hurry, pleased to be chatting on a beautiful day in early summer.

"Are you passing through the village?" Toran was tentative, not wanting to give any suggestion that they were not welcome.

"We've come from much further up the valley, and now we're on our way again." Philip looked across the fields towards the sea.

Toran was unable to hide his curiosity.

"What brought you to our village?"

"There're many routes you can take," said David, "ours led us here."

"We're shepherds" explained Philip, "we tend to follow our instincts, go where the sun or stars lead us."

"Well, that's a coincidence! I found a lamb yesterday when I was walking along the cliffs, lost and no sign of its mother. In fact, I'm about to go and see if it's still where I left it. I'm afraid it may have wandered off, fallen over a precipice, although the dog was to guard…" Toran trailed off, thinking how muddled and incompetent he must sound.

"We shall come with you." David didn't hesitate and Philip nodded. "If we find the little one, we can help you."

"Well…" Toran was struggling with the sudden turn of events, the strangers' quiet confidence that left him no longer in charge. He was not at all sure that he could find the way back to the hut; how foolish he would look if he led these men on a fool's errand.

"We'll follow you," said Philip.

Toran looked at the church as he hesitated. The clock was about to ring out the hour and the stained glass windows glinted in the sunlight. It had stood there for a thousand years, unmoved by the changing vagaries of human life. He took a deep breath.

"I'll lead the way then."

They set off across the fields, heading diagonally towards

the cliff path, where they started to climb, not speaking much as they went, gaining height until the village shrank beneath them. The shepherds were easy companions, walking most of the time in comfortable silence, commenting sometimes on the views or the beauty of the day. When they reached the headland, the full magnificence of the sea made them pause, and they stood gazing down at the waves and across the water towards the horizon. In the far distance, the summit of the island glistened in the sunshine, whilst the waves broke against the rocks at its base in white spray.

"That island stands very much alone," said David. "Does anyone ever go there?"

"Oh no, the currents are treacherous all round it, and, anyway, it's a real refuge for wild life. Trips go out from the harbour further along the coast in summer, but the boats stay well away from its orbit. People around here know only too well the power of the sea. There're many stories about people in the past drowning trying to reach it."

The shepherds stared at the island for a few moments without speaking.

"Let's rest awhile." It was Philip who broke the silence, and Toran nodded gratefully, aware that he was tired and many years older than his companions.

They sat on the headland watching the sea and listening to the sound of the waves and the cries of gulls. Toran glanced at the two men. They seemed so assured, so at peace with their world. He mused about their way of life and their history: where had they come from, how did they find work? He looked upwards, half closing his eyes against the sun's glare. The star still hung there, far out in the depths, pale and solitary. He sensed that the shepherds were aware of its presence, although they said nothing, and he felt a sudden desire to ask them if they knew which star it was and why it was visible now, when all its fellows were hidden from

71

view. Before he could speak, David jumped to his feet.

"Shall we get moving again, see if we can find the lamb?"

Toran nodded, standing up with some effort and looking at the path ahead. He didn't recognise it.

"I'm not sure…"

"Shall I lead the way for a while," suggested David, "the route will become clear."

Thinking back on that walk later, Toran had no idea which path they followed nor how far they walked, but when he was beginning to fear they would never find it the tumbledown hut appeared before them, looking abandoned and neglected. With beating heart, he hurried inside.

"Solace! Solace!"

The gloomy interior was empty, and there was no evidence that either dog or lamb had been there. His heart sank. He should never have left them. He went outside again and looked around in despair.

"They're not here! We'll never find them; they could've gone anywhere." He walked towards the cliff. "Solace!" he called again, but no eager animal came bounding up to greet him.

The shepherds had not joined his search, but stood watching through half-smiling eyes, as if he were the young man, and they his elders.

"I can hear barking," said Philip. "Don't worry, neither the lamb nor dog is lost. Follow us."

Toran shook his head, straining to catch the sound, but to no avail. More disconcerting still, when he searched the cliffs for the way to the sanctuary he could see only the path winding along the headland, surrounded by grasses and wild flowers. It was hopeless. The animals could be anywhere. The shepherds must have been mistaken.

"I think…" he started to say, but he should have had more faith. Within a few minutes of leaving the hut, the bush gleamed ahead of them and, without hesitation, the shepherds started to make their way down the path, not pausing to ask him if they were going the right way. He followed without speaking.

The vastness of the arena caught his breath anew. The brothers were still and silent at his side, gazing around with an intensity that spoke of more than a passing interest. It was the bleating of the lamb that broke the moment, and they laughed to see it standing next to the dog as if this encounter was expected and they were waiting for them. Toran ran across the grass and dropped to his knees, burying his face in Solace's coat, his eyes wet against the warm hair. The animal turned to lay its face against Toran's cheek, whilst the lamb stood by patiently. It was David who swept the tiny creature into his arms, holding it with firm and experienced hands.

"You're strong for such a youngster. I don't think there's anything amiss with you."

"Why isn't it more distressed; why doesn't it seem to be hungry?"

David smiled at Toran.

"I daresay it will drink now," he said, but he offered no explanation, taking the supplies Toran had bought from the shop and going to sit on a rock nearby so he could offer the lamb some milk. Whilst he was gone, Toran put out a bowl of water and a plate of food for Solace but, although the dog ate and drank a little, it did not seem either thirsty or hungry. Philip watched for a moment.

"This is a wise and experienced dog. It doesn't need man for its survival. Come, let's prepare our own food."

Toran was about to say that he did not have enough food for all of them, but Philip was already laying out a loaf of bread, chunks of cheese, fruit, a flagon of red wine and some battered goblets. David joined them, the lamb scampering behind him and, whilst the animals settled down to sleep, the three men seated themselves on the grass. Beside the shepherd's fare, Toran's sandwich looked unappetizing, and he was grateful to tear a chunk from their loaf, accept a piece of cheese. Philip poured the wine into the goblets and, thirsty, Toran raised the drink to his lips, then hesitated. The brothers sat with bowed heads, the food and wine untouched. He felt ashamed. If these men paused to give thanks, why should he be so careless with his gratitude?

"Eat," said David, and Toran took some cheese, savouring the pungent taste.

"And drink," said Philip.

For a while they ate in silence, listening to the whispers of summer. Toran had not known such contentment since Jane's death. Around them, the vast arena seemed to stretch ever further, the semi-circled cliffs rising in sheer walls, guarding the space with breastplates of stone. More than ever, it felt as if they had stumbled upon a secret oasis, undiscovered since the beginning of time. He tried to bring his mind to bear on the present situation.

"What should we do about the lamb?"

David looked at Toran.

"Do?"

"Well, should I take it to one of the farms, see if they have lost one?"

Solace and the lamb still slept side by side, their faces close together, their breathing soft and steady. David put his hand on Toran's arm.

"We'll take care of the lamb."

Toran nodded, but he felt uneasy. How could they look after the lamb if they were moving on to find work? And if they did so, would he lose Solace? He was so engrossed in his own thoughts that he did not realise the shepherds had finished their meal and were watching him. It was Philip's voice that roused him.

"What are you doing here, my friend? What is this place to you?"

"It's the spot where I must build the sanctuary." Toran spoke before he considered his answer, before he knew he was going to blurt out the truth. They did not ask what he meant.

"We shall stay for a while. Perhaps we can help."

Toran trembled.

"I don't really know what I'm meant to do. I just felt this compulsion to find a site. At times I think I'm going mad."

"You are not going mad," murmured Philip. David was staring up at the sky, shielding his eyes against the sun. The star, faint and distant, was still there.

"Who are you?" asked Toran, but they were turning away and did not hear.

"Go home now. Return tomorrow when you're rested. We shall stay here."

Toran realised how exhausted he felt and was glad to obey. He would ask the question again in the morning.

"Solace," he called, but the dog looked at him wistfully, as if saying that he would accompany him if he could, but he must remain behind with the shepherds and the lamb. Toran started to walk across the grass to the path up the cliff.

"And bring your family with you," called Philip.

Toran paused. He couldn't remember mentioning the arrival of the family.

He started to climb. The shepherds watched him until he disappeared from sight.

"Come," said David, "Let's begin. We have a great deal to do before they return in the morning."

Chapter 12

Feeling lonely and strangely apprehensive, Toran walked along the cliff path towards home. He should be jubilant; he had found the place he had been searching for, the shepherds had turned up to help him, and Simon, Catherine and the children were arriving soon. Yet he could not shake off a sense of unease.

The day remained beautiful and he paused to gaze down at the ocean. He could hear waves breaking into the caves beneath his feet and see, far away, the currents surging past the island. Nothing looked any different, but Toran still felt convinced that something had changed. He looked again at the waters below and gasped. That was it! There was something odd about the tide.

He glanced at his watch. The sea should be coming in now, should have turned exactly fifteen minutes ago at low tide. He stared again. From his vantage point he could see clearly: the sea was still surging towards the horizon.

"What's happening?" he whispered. Surely the moon couldn't have altered course in some way? He looked to the sky, searching intently, and felt the skin on the back of his neck tauten and tingle. There was no sign of the moon, not the faintest outline, but the star was still there, and it seemed to have moved closer. More curious still, it appeared deeper in colour, as if something patterned its surface. It must all be his imagination, the tides, the star, or else there was something wrong with his eyes.

He hurried along the path again, trying to close his mind to absurd ideas, attempting to enjoy the loveliness of the day. It was hopeless; nothing was making sense to him, and even finding the arena, the arrival of shepherds, felt bizarre and disturbing. He longed for Jane with her calm and down-to-earth presence. She would laugh gently at him, dispel his wild thoughts. A longing for her swept over him and filled him with such anguish that he cried out aloud and sank to the ground, burying his face in his hands. He couldn't go on any more, struggling on his own like this. He was too old, too tired.

A touch upon his shoulder startled him out of his self-pity, and he leapt to his feet. For just one moment, he thought Jane had returned, for the woman who stood before him had her laughing eyes and pale skin, but he shook his head ruefully as he gazed at her. She was very beautiful, with a mass of fair, curly hair falling to her shoulders, and she was almost as tall as he was, dressed in a rather offbeat way, with a long skirt and a shirt tied round the waist with a cord. It was difficult to tell her age.

"Do you need help?" Her voice was soft and musical, and she smiled at him so kindly that he bit his lips to prevent tears from starting to his eyes.

"I'm fine thanks." How ridiculous he must sound, but she nodded, as if it were quite normal for a seventy-year-old man to be sitting alone on a clifftop in obvious distress. He tried to sound composed, to keep his dignity. "Are you walking the cliff path?"

"I suppose I am."

He noticed then that she carried nothing, not even a small rucksack. Toran felt he was being intrusive, that it was none of his business. He held out his hand.

"My name's Toran. I live in the village quite a way from here, down in the valley."

"Ah." She looked at him as if he had said something fascinating. "I'm Dinitra. I'm just visiting."

"You must take care on these cliffs, they can be dangerous." There was something about this woman that made him feel both protective and uncertain.

"I understand the dangers, but thank you."

"Have we met somewhere before? I feel as if this isn't the first time we've come across one another."

"I think I must have that sort of face. No, I do not think you have seen me before." She shook her head and smiled.

Toran was finding something increasingly unsettling about her. She met his eyes with such directness that it was disconcerting, yet he had no idea what she was thinking. There was nothing at all sensual in her, but it was as if she had lit a fire in him and that, when she was gone, the embers would remain smouldering ready to flare up again.

"I must be going," he said, "my family will be arriving soon. I hope you have a pleasant walk." How absurd he sounded.

"I think we will see each other again."

She was gone before he could speak, moving rapidly up the cliff path the way he had come. He stood for while lost in thought, then set off in the direction of home, anxious now about the time of day; but he had not gone far when he paused, unable to resist turning around to glimpse her once more. She must have made remarkable progress, for there was no sign of her. He sighed; despite her words, he felt sure they would never meet again.

Simon, Catherine and the children had already arrived and were sitting on the wall in front of his cottage enjoying the early evening sunshine. They leapt up to greet him when they saw him hurrying down the lane, laughing off his embarrassed apologies, hugging him affectionately. As Catherine and the children started to unload the car, Simon took his father to one side.

"Do you think there's going to be a war, Dad? Is that why you've sent for us?

"I don't know, Simon, but it may not be as we think."

"So why have you asked us to come?"

"To help me with a great task. I can't manage it alone."

"What task? What's happening?" Simon looked keenly at his father, trying to hide his concern.

He thinks I'm losing my grip, thought Toran, and I can't give him much reassurance at the moment. When he spoke he tried to sound confident.

"Well, I know what I have to do but, I must confess, I'm not exactly sure why I have to do it. Let's go inside and I'll try to explain over a glass of wine."

Simon lifted the last case, and put his arm around his father's shoulders.

"Come on everyone, let's go and see what Grandpa's got for tea!"

Catherine hung back for a moment as the others went into the cottage. Slamming the boot shut she glanced towards the sky. The star hung high above the cottage, hardly visible amongst the deepening pinks and mauves of approaching sunset. She felt as if it had followed them from the north and now waited overhead. Although she knew she was being fanciful she shivered, and quickly followed the family into the cottage.

Chapter 13

The factory was so huge that local folklore said it would take a man a week to walk right around it, and there were rumours that, underground, the same area was dedicated to the most secret research and experiments.

No-one knew how many or who worked there, for the comings and goings were mysterious and closely guarded, and it would be a brave person who questioned what took place inside.

The leader came sometimes and rubbed his hands with pleasure. Progress was well ahead of schedule and, within the next few months, they should be well prepared.

The moon hung over the factory every night as the desert air chilled and blanketed the sand. No-one ever gazed at its light or wondered at its beauty; if they had done so, they might have noticed the unknown star that slipped into the sky and hovered for a while before disappearing, strangely crimson, into the far reaches of the sky.

The fair was very impressive, and the day was kind to the occasion, with blue skies and a soft wind. People from many nations strolled around, drinks in hand, surveying the scene with close interest. The whole function promised to be a profitable and successful event.

"Who's that man?"

One of the organisers was watching a tall, dark-haired visitor who seemed more interested in other attendees than in the gleaming exhibits. His head was unusually small, making his height all the more arresting. His progress amongst the crowd appeared to be smooth and sophisticated.

"No idea, but he'll have been vetted."

The underling shrugged his shoulders. It was not his place to enquire further.

There were many delegations, and the hum of conversations in different languages filled the air, making for a cosmopolitan and cultured atmosphere. As the hours passed by, the sun rose higher and the earth spun towards the west whilst, unnoticed, the pale moon stole into the sky and waited for evening.

Right across the globe, in thousand upon thousand different tongues, people prayed for peace. In great cities, in towns and villages, by the lakesides and sea shores, and at the feet of towering mountains, across the deserts and dusty plains, in remote and hidden valleys, they watched and trembled. Millions stared at their screens hour by hour, or gathered together to find comfort and to share their fear.

"What is the truth?" they asked again and again, but there were no answers.

And so the weeks passed. Some crouched in corners, arms folded across their chests, and stopped up their ears. Others carried on as before, their daily routines creating a fabric of normality. And many millions marched together, holding up their banners of defiance and hope as if they would fill the very skies with their pleas.

High above, crossing untold galaxies, the star travelled towards their tiny world.

Chapter 14

Ellen was not looking forward to the journey. To her surprise, Edward had objected when she told him about the plan, saying he did not want to be taken out of school early, and he had sulked ever since. On reflection, she realised that school was very important to him. As a single parent, working full time and struggling financially, she knew she didn't give him the attention he needed, and his small primary school was a happy and caring environment.

As they left their cramped and dark flat, the sunshine promised another lovely day. Ellen felt her heart lifting at the thought of the sea, and release from the present daily grind of her life. Even Edward smiled with sudden anticipation, and slipped his hand into his mother's.

The train was crowded and already smelt of stale food. Ellen's heart sank. So many of the seats were reserved, and people glanced at them with brief indifference as they struggled down the crowded gangways with their luggage. She was beginning to think that they would have to stand the whole of the four hour journey, when they entered the last carriage where, to her surprise and delight, it was much quieter and there were vacant seats at some of the tables.

"Are these places free?"

The man sitting with his back to the engine by the window was engrossed in a book. He waved a hand.

"Quite free."

Later, Ellen could never be sure how long it was before Edward opened his rucksack and pulled out a comic, a can of lemonade and some biscuits. She was drifting off to sleep, lulled by the motion of the train and the warmth of the sun on her face and, for the first time in weeks, she felt herself relaxing. It was Edward's cries of apology that woke her.

"I'm sorry, I didn't mean to…"

"Oh, Edward!"

She gazed in consternation at the mess on the table, which the boy was desperately dabbing with a grubby tissue. The man's book looked rather damp. He must have stopped reading.

"It doesn't matter." He was smiling as he produced a large handkerchief and started to mop up the spilled lemonade. "I'm always spilling things myself."

Ellen noticed how pale and clear the man's skin was, showing no lines or signs of aging and, because of this, it was difficult to guess how old he might be. At first glance he appeared almost youthful, but when she looked again, it was obvious he was older than she had thought. His eyes were an unusual blue, and they were not young eyes; in fact Ellen felt suddenly shy when she met his candid gaze, and looked away flustered. His hair was almost ash blonde and she suspected that if they stood up, he would tower over her.

When the mopping up was completed, Ellen waited for the man to continue reading his damaged book, or close his eyes. Instead, he smiled at them warmly, as if he were waiting for something to happen. She felt at a loss for words, but Edward had no such inhibitions. The stranger had been kind to him and, as far as the boy was concerned, he was a friend. He looked at the man with wide and troubled eyes.

"Do you think there's going to be a war? Everyone at school says there is, and we'll all be killed."

"Ah, is that what is being said?"

The stranger examined the child keenly, but it was impossible to tell what he was thinking.

"Yes. I'm scared. I haven't got a dad to look after me, it's just mum."

Ellen tried to gather her wits.

"Edward! We could have talked, I didn't know you were worrying." She felt foolish, inadequate. "Grandpa will be able to help."

"Grandpa's old, he needs looking after himself." The boy didn't even glance at his mother in his anxiety to explain how he was feeling. "What's your name?"

"Edward, you mustn't be so rude!" exclaimed Ellen flushing with discomfort, thinking the whole situation was getting beyond her control, but the man raised a slim hand and shook his head.

"That's alright. My name is Michael."

"This is my mum, Ellen, and I'm Edward."

The boy held out his hand and the stranger responded generously, taking the small palm into his own. Without thinking, Ellen stretched out her hand also, and he held it for a moment before releasing it. Suddenly she felt quite tearful, like a child herself, and she turned to face the window so that the sun sparkled on her wet lashes and warmed her skin.

"Do you think there'll be a war?" persisted Edward. "All the kids at school say there will, and I've heard the teachers say so too, when they think we're not listening."

"Where I come from, there are no rumours of war. Try not to be afraid, because being afraid can make you behave in a way that is not good."

"So you don't think we'll all die?"

The boy's face shone with sudden hope. Michael did not reply immediately, but looked out of the carriage window with such intensity that Ellen thought he had not heard the question. She was mistaken, however and, when the answer came, it took her by surprise.

"Do you see that faint star high up in the sky, Edward?"

The boy craned his neck, eagerly scanning the blue and

silver expanse.

"Wow! I've never even noticed a star in the daytime before. I've got an old telescope that Grandpa gave me for my ninth birthday. When I'm staying there, we often look at the sky when it's dark. He knows the names of lots of stars. What star is that?"

"That is a bit of a mystery," said Michael, "but then a bit of mystery can be a very good thing, the right sort of mystery of course."

"But what's...?" began the boy, when the train suddenly sped into a tunnel and, at the same moment, the lights in the carriage went out and the whole place was plunged into darkness.

Edward clutched his mother's hand.

"It's alright, they'll come on again in a moment. Something must have happened when we went into the tunnel."

She was right. Within a short space of time the lights flickered back on and, seconds later, they came out of the tunnel into the sunshine.

The sudden brightness made them blink and it was not until they'd rubbed their eyes that they could see clearly. Michael was no longer sitting opposite them.

"Where's he gone?" cried Edward. "I didn't hear him go, he didn't say anything."

"I'm sure he'll be back in a minute."

"But he's taken his book!"

Ellen's heart sank. The seat opposite looked starkly empty.

"That's what happens on trains. People come and go, and usually you don't notice."

"But Michael was nice."

Ellen tried to comfort him, but she was finding it difficult because, for some reason she felt quite bereft herself. She opened her mouth to suggest they played a game or something, when the train started to shudder and lose speed rapidly until it came to a halt. They were thrown against the back of their seats and could hear loud shouting and hammering against the side of the carriage. Moments later, a voice came over the speaker system telling everyone to remain calm, that there was no danger, but a large demonstration was taking place and people were on the line. Everyone must stay in their seats until further notice.

They looked out of the window at the huge crowds swarming around the train. Even from inside, the atmosphere felt angry and ugly. As they gazed out of the window, they saw a white face close to the glass, and a dark-haired man staring in at them with such venom that Ellen shrank into her seat and put her arm round Edward. For a moment, she thought he might be blind, he had such empty eyes but, a moment later, a fleeting movement of his lips, the flash of a smile, revealed small pebble teeth, and she realised that he was gazing at them with interest.

"Who's that horrid man?"

Ellen shuddered, but kept her voice light. " He can't hurt us, darling. Don't look at him, he'll go away."

At that moment, the guard came into the carriage. He looked surprised when he saw how empty it was.

"You ok?" he asked Ellen.

"There's a rather unpleasant man staring at us through the window. It's frightened my little boy."

The man looked. "No-one there now. These demonstrations bring out all sorts. Started good-naturedly enough but, for some reason, it turned really nasty and some people have been hurt. Funny, when you think they're demanding peace. The police are on their way." He was gone.

"Do you think Michael's there?" Edward gazed out of the window, searching for his new friend.

"We'd never see him amongst all these people, and, anyway, I can't imagine he'd be there."

"Can I walk down the train and look for him?"

"Not on your own!" Ellen spoke more sharply than she intended, but the nature of the demonstration had troubled her, and she felt vulnerable and apprehensive.

"Come with me, mum, please."

"We'll have to wait until we're moving again."

Police had now arrived and were rounding people up, ordering them off the line. Slowly the crowds dispersed, with the injured being helped or carried towards the waiting ambulances. There was no sign of either Michael or the dark-haired man who had stared at them through the window.

The train was starting to move again, and soon the scene was left behind and they were allowed to leave their seats. They walked the length of the carriages, looking from side to side as they went, even waiting outside occupied toilets until the person inside appeared. They went into the buffet car and first class. There was no sign of Michael anywhere.

It was a huge relief when they climbed down from the carriage at last, stiff, sticky and tired, and boarded the little sprinter train that would take them to the coast. They seemed to be the only people going that way, and they had the carriage to themselves. Ellen sighed with pleasure at the sight of the familiar fields, the small lanes and villages, and she started to relax, feeling the tension drain away.

"The sea!" cried Edward, and smiled for the first time since Michael had disappeared. "Are we nearly there?"

"Ten minutes," laughed Ellen.

They jumped onto the platform in the late afternoon sunshine, and put down their luggage. Nothing had changed: pots of brightly coloured flowers stood in front of the railings, and the small building that served as the ticket office and waiting room was riotous with hanging baskets.

Across the other side of the platform the fields stretched into the distance, dotted here and there with grazing cattle and sheep. They could smell the sea. Ellen flung her arms round Edward and gave him a hug. He grinned and hugged her back.

"Where's Grandpa?" He looked around for the familiar figure.

"He must be waiting at the front with the car. Let's go and find him."

Despite her confident words, Ellen felt a tug of concern. Her father was always standing on the platform to meet them, whatever the weather, his face lighting up with pleasure when he saw them.

He was not outside. She looked around in surprise.

"He must have been held up for some reason."

"Now what shall we do!"

"Let's walk. There're never any taxis, and it's only a mile. We'll leave the luggage and collect it later. It'll be quite safe."

"May I help you in some way?"

They spun around in amazement. Michael stood behind them, smiling as if there had been no parting. Edward flung his arms round the man's waist.

"I looked everywhere for you!"

"I know, that is why I am here."

Ellen was so taken aback that she couldn't speak for a moment, but Edward was bursting with excitement.

"Why don't you come with us to Grandpa's? He wouldn't mind."

"Edward!" Ellen found her tongue at last. "I'm sure Michael has other things to do." She heard her own voice, slightly shrill, the words so banal.

"Oh no, I have nothing else to do at the moment. If your mother is happy, I will come with you. Let me take that case."

Ellen felt she was losing control of the situation again, but she nodded and Edward whooped with joy.

"May we talk about the star again?"

They all looked up to where the faint outline of the star hung alone, untouched by any clouds.

"Of course."

The late afternoon had never been more radiant. As they walked together in a landscape rich with early summer, the world seemed wrapped in peace, gathered in a harmony of creation, the air filled with birdsong, gliding gulls, the fields multi-coloured with crops, grazing cattle and sheep, the grasses by the road humming with life. Edward held Michael's hand chatting earnestly, whilst Ellen walked in silence a few steps behind. She did not know what her father would say when they arrived with a complete stranger, but she felt a deep contentment as they walked, and she lifted her head to smell the salt breeze as they drew closer and closer to the sea.

Chapter 15

Shayrath and Ethan worked in silence, all unspoken words held for the moment as they concentrated upon their task. Apart from the rhythmic sound of their labour, the quiet in the barn was so profound that, when the knock upon the door came, they both started in surprise.

"Whoever…?" Ethan looked troubled and turned to his brother.

"No-one comes here!"

A crack of daylight was appearing as the door slowly opened and, within seconds, the sunshine revealed the figure of a tall, swarthy man standing just outside.

"Hello? Anyone around?"

Shayrath leapt to his feet and hurried over. He didn't want a stranger to see the tree. Ethan followed close on his brother's heels.

"Can we help you?"

Shayrath spoke casually, as if it were the most natural thing to turn up at this deserted place and open a door that, as far as he knew, no-one else had ever discovered.

"I've been walking for some time, searching, and found this barn."

"Ah, there's nothing here." Ethan shrugged. "We're about to leave."

The stranger looked over their shoulders.

"But there is something here. What are you doing to the tree?"

The brothers were taken aback. It was difficult to make out the presence of the tree from the doorway, especially in the twilight of the barn.

Shayrath shuffled his feet. He had no intention of giving

any explanation to this man; why, he hadn't even discussed his plans with Ethan.

"Nothing, it's nothing."

Without further comment or asking permission, the man came through the small door and walked over to the tree. The brothers followed, unable to prevent him. He stood for some time gazing at the lifeless form, then knelt to touch the wood.

"We're just stripping the bark, that's all," burst out Ethan.

The man looked up.

"That's a huge task for two people. I'm a carpenter by trade; I'll stay and give you a hand. I've no work at the moment."

"That's kind," Shayrath stumbled over the words in his eagerness to decline the offer, "but my brother's here – we'll soon get it done."

"You'll need more than two people for the work you've in mind. I'll stay. Don't worry, I won't be any trouble. I've got my tools, and I'll shelter in that old cottage if it rains; otherwise I'll sleep outside."

Shayrath nodded, feeling completely outmanoeuvred. He didn't want to leave this stranger alone with the tree. He tried again.

"We've got to be getting home; it won't be very pleasant here on your own. Perhaps…"

"Don't worry. I'll sort myself out." He held out his hand. "I'm Josiah." He smiled warmly. The brothers had no choice.

"We're Shayrath and Ethan."

The man nodded and took their outstretched palms.

"That's settled then. I'll see you tomorrow."

In front of them, the tree seemed vaster than ever, a huge, brooding presence, the trunk thicker than many men's bodies, the branches touching the walls. Reluctantly, the brothers turned to leave, so they did not see Josiah stand unmoving for a few moments, then kneel beside the tree.

It was Shayrath who spoke first.

"Who is that man and how on earth did he stumble on the barn?"

The brothers were walking home in the evening sunshine, in no hurry to reach the house and their mother's mood, enjoying being together again after such a long time.

"It's really odd." Ethan shrugged his shoulders. "He seemed nice enough but, as for how he found us who knows. Everything is a bit odd at the moment; nothing seems to make much sense."

"I tried to stop him!"

"You did! Perhaps he'll be a help in whatever it is we're doing?"

"I promise I'll try and explain. But first, tell me, why have you come back, Ethan? Are you on the run? What's happened?"

"In some ways I feel like a deserter, but I'm not on the run. If I tell you what's happened, you'll find it difficult to believe."

"Tell me."

It was a relief to pour out the story: the loss of his unit, the sudden change in scenery from wasteland to beauty, the climb up the mountain, the encounter in the woods and his desperate flight. His dismissal from the army. Shayrath listened intently, never uttering a word until Ethan paused for breath.

"Why did you run? What frightened you so much?"

"I thought I was losing my mind, hallucinating. Yet it seemed so real, I was terrified."

Shayrath was about to ask another question when he

noticed a plume of silver-grey ahead.

"Is that smoke?"

"It could be!" Ethan hurried forward and cried out in astonishment.

The travellers were sitting around their camp fire as if they had been settled there for a long time. The same battered pan exuded its enticing smell, and the old piebald horse grazed on the sparse tufts of grass nearby.

"Good evening." It was the youngest gypsy who spoke, his deep voice relaxed and warm. "Glad to see you made the journey safely. Why don't you and your brother join us."

"How do you... how have you...?"

The men shook their heads, beckoning them to sit on the stools close to the fire.

"We should be going." Shayrath was torn between curiosity and a compulsion to stay, and the thought of his mother waiting for them at home.

"Time enough," said one of the older gypsies, smiling and handing them each a goblet of wine which smelt of herbs and spices. "Drink."

How long they sat there, neither of them knew. No-one spoke, and the silence gathered them close and let them rest until the sky started to glow with approaching sunset, then turned to charcoal as the stars appeared. Ethan gazed at the changing patterns above.

"It's closer," he whispered.

"It seems so to you at the moment," said the youngest gypsy. "It'll be closer yet when the time comes."

"Why are you here? Where are you travelling?"

"We'll leave when the hour demands. Remember, both of you, to keep watch when we're gone."

The brothers were growing sleepy with the effect of the wine and the warmth from the fire. After a while they rose to leave. The gypsies smiled in farewell, and started to move around the camp, their silhouettes of uncertain shape and purpose, while the old piebald horse could have been a stag or a unicorn, so mysterious were the shadows of that night.

Shayrath and Ethan found themselves coming to the outskirts of town, with little recollection as to how they had arrived there. As they walked, Ethan had told his brother about his journey home after he'd been dismissed from the army, the demonstration and carnage, meeting the gypsies. He didn't mention the man who had sat staring at him through hidden eyes that morning; the memory still made him shudder with distaste.

"It's almost as if those gypsies are following me. I don't understand."

"It's very odd." Shayrath looked uncertain. "And where's the rest of their tribe?"

Neither brother spoke for a few moments, lost in thought, struggling for explanations.

"The demonstration I talked about. People were protesting at the rumours of another war. Lots were killed. Did you hear about it?"

"Nothing. You know how news is suppressed. But there's talk of another war here. It mustn't happen again!"

"The army seemed to be preparing for something big, but we were never told. Our poor people."

"Maybe there's a chance something will stop it."

"Tell me now, Shayrath, tell me what you're up to in the barn; is it something to do with the threats all around us?"

"I'll try and explain but, as you said, nothing seems to make sense at the moment. It's ever since I noticed that star…"

The two men had been so engrossed in their conversation that they did not hear the shouts in the distance but, as

Shayrath began to speak, the noise increased, and they looked ahead in surprise. Crowds of people were pouring out onto the street, shouting in dismay to one another and, when the brothers reached the market place, the square was packed with jostling people.

They could not believe they'd been so oblivious, and they gasped aloud, staring overhead in disbelief. The sky was ablaze with colour. The moon glowed fiercely, and the stars were shot through with crimson and purple, the black clouds alive with flames which twisted and turned as if dancing to some unknown choreography of the firmament. Dominating everything was the stranger star, larger than ever and, even as they gazed, it seemed to move beyond the face of the moon and draw closer. The enigmatic script could be seen burning on its surface. Shayrath and Ethan gripped each other's hands.

"Help us!" A young woman was standing close by, holding a baby in her arms. "People are saying a huge bomb's been dropped and we're all going to die."

"It's alright, it's alright." Ethan put his arm around the shoulders of the terrified girl. "It's not a bomb; it's something happening way above us. Look, the sky's already changing, returning to normal."

He was right. The colours were fading even as they watched, and the stranger star appeared to grow smaller, the writing on its surface disappearing as if someone had closed the pages of a book. With one voice, the crowd groaned with relief. The girl turned to Ethan.

"Thanks. I panicked for a moment...the baby" and she was gone, disappearing amongst the hordes of people.

"Poor kid, so young. Wonder why she was on her own."

Shayrath looked at his brother, his face etched with concern.

"What's happening to us? I'm afraid."

"So am I. Do you really think the task you're about will make any difference?"

"I don't see how it can, but we must carry on. And Josiah has turned up; as you said, perhaps he'll be a help. There's nothing else we can do but carry on. We're powerless."

"Oh Shayrath, neither of us knows anything." They had left the square and were walking down one of the few well maintained avenues in town. "I see the President's palace is as well guarded as ever." They paused to look at the grey edifice surrounded by high railings, where soldiers stood every few yards, their rifles at the ready.

"That won't do him much good in the end." The wind was rising, and dust rose from the pavement, ghost of the distant desert, and blew into their eyes. "We'd better get on home. Goodness knows what state mother will be in."

Ethan nodded and they started to trudge along the road, despondent and tired. The moon shone over them and stars littered the sky. Far away, hardly visible now, the unknown star hung alone, a pale spectre against the darkness of night.

Chapter 16

Toran knew he had forgotten something important, but he could not remember what it was, his mind was so filled with a mixture of apprehension and excitement. The arrival of Simon, Catherine and the children had been a great relief at first, and the joy of seeing them after so many months had taken him through the first hour with a glow of pleasure, but the atmosphere changed when Catherine went upstairs to start unpacking. Lachlan switched on the television and, before the adults realised what was happening, the early evening news invaded the room, images flashing across the screen of starving children, of people fleeing, and the newscaster speaking in a monotone about the likelihood of war spreading across the globe. Toran switched off the programme, but the damage was done. Pale-faced and a little tearful, Joquella went upstairs to find her mother, whilst Lachlan wandered outside and could be seen sitting on the small wall in front of the cottage.

"Why've you sent for us, Dad?" Simon looked anxiously at his father. "What's going on?"

Toran took a deep breath and tried to explain, pouring out the events of the last months, relieved to tell someone at last what had been dominating his thoughts for so long. As he spoke of Solace and the lamb, of the shepherds and finding the huge arena above the sea, he felt his son staring at him with concern. He hadn't mentioned the star at first, the story sounded so fanciful but, as he went on, he knew he couldn't leave it out, and he faltered as he tried to describe the effect on him when he caught his first glimpse one night, his sense of foreboding and the compulsion to begin his search. He stopped speaking at last, and sat in anticipation of Simon's reaction to the story.

"Nothing you say makes sense, Dad, but then, nothing does make sense at the moment. Catherine's been very upset lately, which is so unlike her. She had some sort of vision the other day which terrified her. Later she thought that perhaps what she saw was a possibility, not a certainty. And I…" Simon hesitated, then told his father about his walk up the mountain with the children, of the myth handed down by the old people in the village, of how the eagle had watched them, only disappearing when they first heard the sound of water, and of finding the spring running clear where no water had been seen in living memory.

Toran went to his son and placed a hand on the younger man's shoulder. Simon put his arms around his father's waist and laid his head against his chest. They felt in that embrace the love they found difficult to express in words, and the comfort of shared apprehension rooted in the values they both held so dear.

"The star," said Toran, "I've never seen a star like it before and, at times, it seems to be getting closer."

Simon stood up and kissed his father on the forehead.

"We've seen it too. It sounds absurd, but I feel it's waiting…"

The sounds of voices outside stopped him in mid-sentence, and both men hurried to the window.

"It's Ellen and Edward!" cried Toran. "I'm going mad, I knew there was something I had to do. Poor darlings, what must they think of me?"

"Don't worry." Simon was looking amused and surprised. "Ellen seems to have found herself a friend and, I must say, he's very handsome."

"Grandpa!" Edward bust into the room, followed by Lachlan, and flung his arms around Toran.

"Why weren't you at the station? We had an awful journey until we met Michael, and then we thought he'd gone, but he hadn't and please, please may he stay as well?"

"Edward!" laughed Ellen, who stood behind her son, stretching out her arms to her father.

Toran took her hand and drew her close, and Simon came to put his arms around the small group, gathering Lachlan into the circle as he did so. They stood for a few moments, feeling the joy of being together and, a moment later, Catherine and Joquella came into the room with cries of pleasure, and flung their arms around the others.

"Oh goodness, I've forgotten Michael; whatever will he think of me!" gasped Ellen suddenly. "Everyone, come and meet Michael. He's been so kind to us."

Outside, the first hints of dusk were creeping into the air as the sun slipped lower, and shadows lengthened across the roofs of cottages and cooled the earth. Michael stood waiting quietly, gazing to where the star hung alone, faint against the distant blue. He turned when he heard them coming.

"Oh, please forgive me!" cried Ellen. The man smiled, shaking his head, as Toran stepped forward to clasp his hand, introducing him to everyone as he did so.

"Ellen says you've been so kind. You must think she has a very unloving father!" He hesitated, feeling foolish, inept in front of this tall stranger who looked at him with such understanding. "Please do stay to eat with us. It's a very simple meal I'm afraid, but you're so welcome."

"Thank you," said Michael.

Toran opened his mouth to ask their visitor if he were staying locally but hesitated, thinking the question might sound intrusive.

"Oh good." Catherine smiled with pleasure. "Let's go and eat."

Lachlan and Joquella followed their mother into the cottage, Simon and Ellen close behind. Toran gestured to Michael, but the man turned to Edward.

"Will you show me the way?"

The boy had not gone with the others. Now, he held out his hand, and Michael took it with such a natural grace that Toran could have wept for the fatherless child.

It was a happy meal although, later, Toran could not remember seeing Michael eat anything. His plate had been empty when they cleared the dishes, so he must have done so, but he certainly refused a second helping, much to the relief of the children, who finished every morsel and declared they were still hungry. As if by common consent, the conversation remained light and cheerful; there was no discussion about the purpose of the gathering, nor any mention of the following day and how they might spend it. Michael spoke little, but his quiet and thoughtful presence encouraged harmony.

"You're going to stay the night aren't you?" pleaded Edward when the meal was finished and Ellen and Simon had gone into the kitchen to make tea. "You could sleep on the sofa – Grandpa wouldn't mind."

Toran opened his mouth to extend an invitation, although he was a little perturbed at the thought, but the words were never uttered.

"There's something going on outside," called Simon, "there seems to be some sort of firework display and lots of villagers are already on the street. You said nothing about fireworks, Dad."

"Fireworks!" Lachlan and Joquella were on their feet in an instant. "Come on everyone!"

Catherine, Simon and Ellen jumped up to follow, but Toran did not stir, and Edward remained sitting next to

Michael.

"It's not fireworks is it Michael? Who are you?"

"I have travelled a long way to find you. Come, we need to go outside."

The sky was ablaze with colour. The moon glowed fiercely, and the stars were shot through with crimson and purple, the black clouds alive with flames which twisted and turned as if dancing to some unknown choreography of the firmament. Dominating everything was the stranger star, larger than ever and, even as they gazed, it seemed to move beyond the face of the moon and draw closer. The enigmatic script could be seen burning on its surface.

"My God," whispered Toran, drawing Joquella close and looking around for the others.

"What's happening, Grandpa?" He could feel the girl's body trembling and she clutched his hand.

"I'm not sure darling, but it'll be alright."

Simon and Catherine appeared, looking shocked and afraid, with Lachlan close to his father. Simon gripped Toran's arm.

"The star! We must get people to safety."

The street was full of frightened villagers, calling out their astonishment and fear to one another.

"That star's going to crash and kill us all!" yelled a young man, who was staring at the sky with horror.

Toran recognised the farm worker he'd seen in the shop, the one who had been so vocal about the need for war.

"The star won't crash; it's an illusion that it seems so close." It was the priest who spoke. Toran knew him well and liked and respected him. His task was an unenviable one, trying to run six churches in the surrounding villages, with shrinking congregations. "Try to stay calm. It's the result of something a long way away and will pass."

Despite the brave words, Toran saw the man cross himself

and close his eyes briefly and, a moment later, he felt a touch on his shoulder and turned to see the priest standing next to him.

"The church?" Toran asked.

"Yes, let's take everyone there for shelter. Hopefully, people will feel in less danger inside such a solid building." He raised his voice. "We're going to the church for shelter. It'll be safe there."

They were desperate to believe him. Young and old, babes in arms and children, the sick and vulnerable, followed the priest, urging and helping each other along, making their way towards the graveyard.

"Edward!" Toran heard the desperate voice of his daughter. "Edward!" She was next to him a moment later. "Dad, Edward has disappeared; I thought he was with Simon and the others."

Toran looked around, but there was no sign of the boy.

"He must be with Michael. You go on into the church; I'll go back and find him."

"You can't do that. I'll come with you."

"Go with your brother. It'll be alright." He gave her a gentle push. "Simon, take Ellen with you. I won't be a moment," and he was gone before either of his children could argue with him.

The village street was deserted, and many of the cottage doors were open with lights left on inside. Toran's own front door was ajar, and he found Edward sitting in the small front room by the window, pale and miserable, with traces of tears on his cheeks.

"Michael's gone. He said I would see him again, but I don't believe him."

Toran knelt in front of his grandson and took his face between his hands.

"Michael would never lie to you. If he said you'd see him

again, you will."

"He told me to try not to be afraid, that being frightened can make you behave in a bad way. Do you think that's true, Grandpa?"

"It certainly can be. It's a bit of a mystery, what's happening at the moment."

"Michael said the right kind of mystery can be a good thing sometimes," whispered Edward. "Do you think that's true as well?"

Toran looked out of the window and saw that the star was moving away, the script on its surface growing fainter.

"Yes, I do. Look, the sky's already changing colour and fading. Let's go to the church and find the others. They're all there."

He took the boy's hand, and together they walked out of the cottage and along the street. The star was moving into the upper reaches as darkness returned.

"I'm not scared, Grandpa."

"You're a good, brave boy. I'm proud of you."

Edward smiled.

They were nearly at the entrance to the graveyard, and they paused for a moment by the gate. Toran listened intently. He could hear the waves breaking on the shore, and knew from their sound that the tide was receding. He glanced up at the moon. The waters should have been rising at this hour. He shivered, clasping Edward's hand tighter as they headed for the church.

Chapter 17

It was another glorious day, and the cliff path had never seemed so enticing, nor the sea such magnificent shades of emerald and blue. In the distance, the island appeared to float on the water like a lost kingdom from an ancient world, the rocks turrets of silver, the caves at its base, eyeless windows into another realm.

There had been little conversation as they travelled; perhaps it was the beauty of the day which silenced them, although Toran suspected that it was the memories of the previous evening which were making everyone thoughtful and disinclined to speak. Even the children didn't exchange their usual banter, so that the cry of the gulls and the waves washing onto the cliffs below vied with the sounds of crickets for dominance. No-one asked Toran the purpose of their expedition, although they had brought a picnic with them, suspecting they would be gone for some time.

"Look!" Lachlan's cry broke the silence. "There's someone up there on the path. What do you think he's doing?" He looked at his grandfather.

"He may be waiting for us."

"We didn't know we'd be meeting anyone else."

"I didn't have time to explain anything last night. You never know who you might meet on these paths."

"Do you think it's Michael?" Edward's voice was eager with hope. "He said I'd see him again."

"That man's dark haired and shorter, but I'm sure you'll see Michael soon." Toran took his grandson's hand. "Come on."

No-one asked any more questions. They climbed steadily for some time, Simon leading the way, until they reached the figure on the cliff, where Simon paused, uncertain what to do. The shepherd stood waiting, relaxed in the midday sunshine. He showed no surprise at seeing seven people, but held out his hand and smiled with pleasure.

"I'm David. It's good to see you. Follow me, please."

"Where're we going?" Lachlan looked at the man, intrigued and curious. "It's just endless cliff tracks up here."

"Ah. I'm a shepherd. We're off to find a lamb that's lost its mother."

Joquella and Edward looked delighted, whilst Ellen and Catherine turned to Toran in surprise.

He nodded.

They walked behind him along the path, with no idea of how long they journeyed, climbing until the breaking of waves was a distant murmur, and the horizon indistinguishable from the sea. At last, ahead, they saw a bush which gleamed in the sunlight, and here David paused.

"Take care," he said.

Following the shepherd's lead, they made their way down the steep and narrow path, the children exclaiming with excitement, until they reached the bottom and saw spread out before them the vast arena.

Simon took his father by the arm, gazing around in awe and disbelief.

"How did you find this place? I've never seen it on any map, nor referred to by the villagers. How has such a huge area been carved out of the cliff face?"

"It's surprising what people can walk past without noticing," said David, before Toran could speak. "Where you stand now was always there to be discovered."

They stood for a long time, trying to take in the scale and magnificence of the arena, at a loss to know how to respond, or understand what they should do. Edward's shout broke the silence.

"Michael!"

It was he, tall and still, white-haired against the light, standing with his back to the waters, staring at the sky. Edward raced across the grass, then stopped in front of the motionless figure and held out his hand. Michael took it, then placed his other hand on the boy's head.

So engrossed was he in the scene, it took Toran a few moments to realise that another person stood quietly by, waiting for the moment to make her presence known.

"Dinitra?" He hesitated, for there was something different about her which he could not identify. How could he have imagined yesterday that he knew her from some other place? "It is Dinitra, isn't it?"

She inclined her head and smiled.

"Ah, quite a gathering," said Philip, who stood with his brother waiting to greet them. "It's a fine beginning."

Toran introduced the family to the shepherd and Dinitra, stumbling a little as he wondered how to explain this meeting in a way that would make any sense to anyone, when he couldn't explain it to himself. It was Solace who broke the moment, appearing suddenly with the lamb close by his side. Toran exclaimed with pleasure as the dog came and pressed its head against his side, then returned to stand by the lamb which stood on its own, waiting.

Joquella went and knelt on the ground, trying to put her arms around the tiny creature, which slipped from her grasp and stood at a little distance watching her. The girl laughed, but Simon saw that Catherine was observing the scene with a worried frown on her forehead, and he slipped his arm through hers. He knew what she was remembering.

"She's alright," he whispered.

"Come, we have food laid out ready," called Philip.

Toran and Simon hung back for a moment as the others obeyed the summons.

"What's going on, Dad? You told me you'd been searching for this place over many months. What did you plan to do when you found it?"

"I thought I would build a sanctuary," said Toran ruefully. "I'd even tried to design it. A place where people could find shelter and safety. I know now what an impossible dream that was, but I do believe that all this has some meaning. We'd better join the others."

No-one expressed surprise at the food laid out on the ground, and they added their own picnic to the meal without speaking. Nor did anyone question the pause before they ate; even the children seemed to understand the imperative to give thanks, and that the strange words were a prelude to a very special feast. The loaves of bread looked newly baked, the large round of cheese straight from a farm, and the piles of fruit must have been collected early that morning, they shone so freshly in the warm light. Philip poured the red wine from a stone flask into the goblets, handing one to everyone, including the children.

"Eat," said David as he tore the loaves into pieces and offered them around, "and drink," he added, as Dinitra cut the cheese and gestured that they should help themselves.

If they lived to be a thousand years old, they would never share a meal like this one. The grasses were entwined with wild flowers, and the scent filled the air with summer. Above, the gulls circled and floated on the breeze, apparently indifferent to the temptation of the food beneath them. The sky spun out towards an ever deeper blue, and not a single cloud passed in front of the sun. White horses rode out beyond the island, surrounding it with a barrier of foaming surf.

Philip and David leant against each other's backs as they ate, with Solace and the lamb close by. Lachlan and Joquella rested near their parents, while Toran sat by the shepherds watching the scene and enjoying the wholesome fare. Dinitra seemed to have taken Edward under her wing, and the boy sat next to her munching his food with obvious satisfaction, although he kept on glancing over at Michael, who stood a little apart, his white-blonde hair illuminated in the sunshine, his face slightly in shadow. His slender fingers clasped a goblet, but Toran could not be sure if he drank from it, nor if he ate any of the bread which he held in his other hand. He seemed to be listening intently, as though behind the cry of gulls and sound of breaking waves, he heard something quite different.

If he could have suspended time, Toran would have sat there until twilight, the sun warming his head, the sound of water lulling him to drowsiness, the simple food satisfying in a way no other meal could be, the wine melting in his mouth, as if all the flowers around had been gathered into one bouquet and prepared for his delight. His family was safe beside him, and the four strangers brought a sense of peace, the lifting of a great burden. Even the animals, still slumbering, offered hope.

Lachlan had finished his bread and cheese, and sat munching an apple. Toran saw the shepherds watching the boy, their expressions impossible to interpret.

"Did you see the sky last night?" he asked. "Everyone rushed to shelter in the church. People were saying a war had started, and that some country had dropped a massive bomb."

"It was horrible," whispered Joquella, "I hid in the vestry."

"I felt so sorry for the children. Lots were crying, and their parents looked so scared." Ellen could not help speaking, although she had not meant to. "And the old people. What would happen if…?" To her embarrassment, she felt tears springing to her eyes, and she could say no more.

"It's alright now." Catherine put her arm round Joquella's

108

shoulders, "but it certainly was a spectacular sunset."

Simon jumped to his feet and looked around.

"What are we doing in this place? How can we build a sanctuary here? Who would find it and, if they could, what would be the use of it?"

"I was thinking of some kind of cathedral," said Toran ruefully. "But that's impossible. I don't know how I ever thought it could be done."

Michael had not spoken for a long time, but now he looked at them all for a few moments, compassion and understanding on his face.

"A sanctuary can be for the heart and soul as well as the body, and a building can shut people out as well as offer shelter."

"Shall we go down to the beach and try to build an ark, like Noah did?"

"Oh, Joquella!" Lachlan shook his head.

"I know!" cried Edward. "Let's build a shelter for the lamb. Then, if it rains, it'll be dry."

His cousins laughed, but Philip and David smiled at the boy.

"That's an interesting idea, Edward." David waved his arm towards the towering cliff. "We could make it over there. It wouldn't take long."

The shepherds looked towards Michael.

"A shelter for the lamb would be a good beginning. You have all been called here to attempt a task and all of you have answered that call. For the moment, that is enough."

"How is it we're here? What do you want of us?" Simon was almost shouting in vexation.

"It is not what I want. Your father wished to build a sanctuary and that is a good thing. If it is built with the right foundations, its effect will be profound." There was something in the man's voice that quietened Simon, made

109

him feel that he was missing the point, but that he was not being judged for doing so. He felt bewildered and uncertain, and could only shake his head.

The shepherds gathered the children around them and explained their plans, giving each one a job. The three listened carefully, enthusiastic to begin their work.

"Come with us," said David, heading for the cliffs, and the youngsters were gone, chattering with anticipation. Solace and the lamb followed.

"Shall we help?" Toran suggested.

Ellen and Catherine nodded, but Simon looked dubious.

"What Michael says, it makes no sense, but…"

"You feel you can trust him?" said his father.

"I do trust him, I don't know why, but I still can't understand what he says. It's alright for the children to be building a little shelter with the shepherds, but surely we should be doing something much more active: banging on the doors of parliament, demonstrating, demanding peace." Catherine slipped her arm into his.

"Why don't we join in for now? It'll be a relief to be doing something. We can talk later."

Dinitra had been standing listening. Now she spoke.

"I think what Catherine says makes sense, Simon. Join the others for now and, later, things will be much clearer for you."

He nodded, though he looked close to tears.

Michael watched them walk across the grass towards the cliffs. He turned to look at the sea, and the star hovering high up in the sky, above the island.

"It is several hours till darkness," he murmured. "Let us make the most of the light."

Chapter 18

Although it was well past midnight, Ethan could not rest. The events of the day kept flashing through his mind and, every time he closed his eyes, he saw the sky ablaze with strange light, and the star drawing nearer.

Shayrath appeared to be in a deep sleep. They had not drawn the curtains and the night sky looked tranquil, the moon shining through the glass with such intensity that Ethan could imagine climbing onto the roof and touching its face. He glanced at his watch. It was one in the morning; he knew he would still be awake at dawn and the thought was intolerable. Without realising his own intentions, he slid out of bed, threw on his clothes and crept from the room.

The streets were ribbons of shadowy grey, and nothing stirred to witness Ethan's hesitant steps through the town. The President's summer palace rose in forbidding grandeur as he approached. When it had been built, long before the first brutal war, it must have been a beautiful location. Before the desecration and droughts, the growing poverty of the people, this town had been a place of fine avenues and leafy trees, the countryside unspoiled, the desert a distant whisper. Presidents still used the palace a few weeks of the year, but they were never seen out amongst the inhabitants. Now, soldiers stood outside the gates and at regular intervals along the high walls, while bright lights arched across the area. The current President was in residence. Ethan could just identify silhouettes of grey clad figures in the watch towers, and the west wing windows were lit up, although the rest of the building was shrouded in darkness. Somebody must be working late into the night.

He was about to move on when the great iron gates began

to open, and he shrank against a tree, pulling his jacket close about his face so that no reflection from his skin could attract attention. The soldiers stood rigid as two large limousines glided through the opening. Ethan watched them disappear down the road; what was going on in such secrecy at this hour? He waited a few moments, then stole away.

Night engulfed the familiar daytime landscape, and patterned it into unknown territory. Straggling vegetation lurked at his feet, the sluggish river crawling beside him like some creature of the deep, its back pock-marked with weed and debris. The light of the moon had faded and, when he looked up at the sky, he saw that it was pinned behind a bank of clouds, its face masked and obscured. There was no sign of the star. Ethan fought down his growing unease; perhaps he should turn back.

He stood for a few minutes, full of indecision, then shook his head; he would not be a coward and slink home. He had left determined to go and speak to the gypsies, wake them up if necessary, and ask them all the questions that swirled in his head. Perhaps they knew something about the tree. He loved and respected his brother, but the work on it seemed pointless and exhausting. What did Shayrath think he was doing, as the rumours of war grew, and people right across their fragile planet longed only for peace?

He was drawing closer to the spot where the travellers had made their camp. Even though it was the middle of the night, he hoped that they would be awake, sitting around the fire, keeping watch. He sniffed expectantly for the familiar smell of burning wood, peering through the darkness for a glimpse of the caravan. He hurried forward, wondering if he could call out but, with each step, his heart sank further.

They were gone. The ashes from the fire were as cold as morning dew, and the caravan and piebald horse might never have visited that lonely spot. Ethan shivered. He felt vulnerable, far from any human contact. The darkness seemed to intensify, and he looked around nervously, expecting some form to emerge from the shadows. He should never have come. What would Shayrath think if he woke up and found him gone?

He turned towards the path, full of dread at the thought of the walk back to town, determined not to glance over his shoulder or listen for the tread of unknown feet. He had gone some way when a ray of light fell on his face, and he could see. He gasped with relief; the moon had appeared again, and would guide him. He looked up. There was no moon, but the star hung behind him dominating the sky and, without hesitation, he started to move in the opposite direction from town, following the light without giving any thought as to where he was being led. He was so intent on not going astray, that it was some time before he realised that he was heading towards the barn, and he was almost upon the building before he knew where he was.

The tell-tale scent of smoke told him that the gypsies had arrived some time before him. They were sitting around the fire murmuring in quiet voices, and Josiah sat with them, looking relaxed and peaceful. Even as Ethan watched, a fifth man appeared out of the shadows and joined the others round the fire. Tall and slim, it was impossible to see his face, but his hair was thick and long, and he was casually dressed. The others showed no surprise at his presence, as if he had been with them for some time, or that they already knew him from another place.

Ethan was so mesmerized by the scene before him, that he was unaware of someone creeping up behind, and it was not until he felt a hand on his arm that he knew he'd been discovered. He spun round, ready to defend himself. It was Shayrath.

"I saw the star, and guessed you'd be here," he whispered.

"Oh Shayrath, I'm so relieved you've come. Do you see that another man's joined them? What's going on? I think I saw the President leaving the palace as I passed. I'm afraid."

"Why don't you join us?" The voice was deep and rich; it could have been the youngest gipsy speaking, or even the stranger. The brothers looked at each other, uncertain, then walked slowly towards the fire, and stood just outside the circle. "You've no need to be afraid. We are gathering, and you have found us."

"Tell us what's going on!" cried Ethan. "Gathering for what? There's so few of us. What do you want of Shayrath and me?"

"Carry on your work as you have been doing. This is Matthew. He's come to help." The man nodded and smiled at the brothers.

"Carving up an old tree that's been dead goodness knows how long!" burst out Ethan,. "How's that going to change anything!"

"Ethan!" Shayrath looked distressed.

Josiah stirred, but it was Matthew who spoke.

"You're not alone, and you can't change events through protests or violence now. Your way is gentle. Follow that path."

"What path!" Ethan was in despair.

"The path you are following now."

"Our people? All people? Is there a chance they can be safe after all?" Desperate with longing, Shayrath struggled to find the right words, and fell silent. The youngest gypsy beckoned the brothers to join them round the fire.

"There is a time for everything, and a season for all things," he said, and handed them each a goblet of the warm wine.

Shayrath and Ethan walked home, both lost in thought, and it was not until they reached the town that they turned to each other in consternation. Despite the hour, many people were on the streets and, outside the President's palace, a huge crowd was chanting "Where are the shelters" whilst the soldiers held up their rifles menancingly.

"What's going on?" Ethan grabbed the arm of a man nearby. "What are all these people doing?"

"Where've you been?" The man stared at him in disbelief. "Didn't you hear the sirens! People came rushing out to go to the shelters, but there's only signs, no shelters."

He was gone.

"That man's right." Shayrath shook his head. "I don't think there are any shelters, not for people like us anyway."

Ethan thought of the crowds he'd seen running for their lives, trying to escape the carnage in that unknown town.

"I believe you. It's probably a false alarm, for now, but it must've been terrifying."

"If what the gypsies seem to be saying is true, maybe we won't need any shelters," said Shayrath, and Ethan shrugged his shoulders.

"We'd better be getting home. Mother!"

On the horizon, a shaft of light suggested the beginning of dawn. Their time around the camp fire seemed far away, and the peace of those moments lost in the clamour of the streets. They trudged towards the house, hoping that their mother might have slept through the noise and chaos.

She was awake, sitting in the kitchen, a shadowy figure half hidden by darkness, wearing her nightclothes and clutching a knife. Their hearts melted with pity. Shayrath was about to say how sorry they were to have left her, when they heard the purr of aircraft, many of them, flying in from the west. Ethan caught his mother's hand, yelling at her to get under the table, but, so loud was the noise, his voice was lost in the roar of the onslaught.

Chapter 19

Toran was in the shop once again, buying supplies. The atmosphere in the village had changed overnight, and the placed buzzed with conversation and speculation. The time spent together in the church, the fear that they might die, had shaken people out of their everyday complacency, and arguments and rivalries were forgotten as people turned to each other and admitted their vulnerabilities.

The church that night seemed to take on a new character. The village population was just under eight hundred, but only a handful went to worship on a Sunday, and Toran had usually been one of a tiny congregation. On bleaker days, he had felt dispirited, as if he were taking part in an irrelevant ritual. He had always loved the place, but its struggle to be heard often left him sad and lonely after the service.

All that had been transformed. As a sanctuary, the building was no longer a still and lifeless edifice of stone, ignored by most of the villagers, but had become a place of refuge, welcome and permanence. They had not dared to switch on the lights, but the glow from the sky had lit up the shadowy interior, so that the cross on the altar sparkled, and the stained-glass windows gave out their richly coloured stories. Toran could have sworn he had heard many thousands of footsteps on the uneven stones, and felt the breath on his face of those he could not see. He had glanced around, wondering if others shared his sense of generation upon generation coming here in times of crisis. It was impossible to know, but many had fallen silent as the priest prayed for their deliverance from danger and, on his way to the shop, when he'd taken his usual route to stand by Jane's grave for a few moments, he'd noticed a couple of villagers slipping into the church.

He hurried to choose the few items he needed, exchanging friendly words with others as he did so, but he was anxious to waste no time and, within a few minutes, he was at the till. The shopkeeper greeted him with a smile.

"Another perfect day - makes you wonder when it'll end though, after last night." There was a question in the man's voice, an underlying fear. Toran tried to reassure him.

"I've a feeling that things might change, something happen to give us hope."

"Hope?"

"I try to remember those words when I'm really low." Toran hesitated, then carried on. "About power being given to the weak and strength to the powerless. It doesn't seem much like it at the moment, but I guess those old prophets understood more than I do!"

The man grunted. "It'd need a miracle!"

Toran nodded.

A few moments later, he was on his way to the cliff path. He wanted to join the family as soon as possible, and they'd set off some time ago, urged by the children, who were keen to get on with their project. He must be at least an hour behind them.

There was another reason why he was in a hurry. Edward had come to him early that morning, his eyes bright with excitement.

"Grandpa, I've got a great idea. Can some of the children in the village go with us and help build the shelter for the lamb. I bet they'd love to."

"Oh, Edward, I'm not sure that's possible. We'd have to ask their parents and…"

"So long as Mum and Simon and Catherine are there."

"The shepherds?"

"They'd be happy, I know they would. Please, Grandpa."

Toran had hesitated, reluctant to disappoint the boy, but dubious that it was a wise idea. He'd opened his mouth to say it wasn't possible when he'd glanced out of the window and seen a group of about ten children waiting in the sunshine. He knew them all: one of the boys struggled at school and could be a real problem for the teachers, while the youngest girl had been very upset when her parents divorced, and had retreated into herself.

"Edward!"

"Michael wouldn't mind!"

"Michael hasn't got to make sure they all make it safely up that cliff path!"

"But he will. I know he will!"

Toran smiled to himself as he walked. In a way he still didn't quite understand, the plan had fallen into place, and he'd watched the group leave for the arena, chatting and laughing as if they were off for any ordinary outing. He'd been outmanoeuvred.

He had always loved walking on these cliffs but, today, he felt as though he were passing through a land untouched by any human presence other than his own. As he climbed, he saw the island across the sea, shrouded with sunshine, so that the summit disappeared into a crown of light, and the star, paler than wisps of clouds, hung high above. The tide was rising, as it should be at this hour, and the world felt at peace. He sighed.

When the shadow fell across his face, he was taken by surprise. The sun had disappeared for the moment, turning the ocean to a sombre grey and hiding the island in mist. He shivered. How could things change in an instant?

"Hello there, pleasant day, isn't it."

He had been so convinced he was on his own that he had

difficulty in not exclaiming aloud. The man sprawled on the grass in front of him seemed friendly enough, but Toran took a step backwards. His head was small for his body, and the eyes seemed to have sunk into their sockets and glittered dully, as if he were ill. It looked as though he had plastered his black hair with oil, and his skin was the colour of chalk, his lips thin and moist.

"Yes, indeed it is," said Toran, and he made to walk by as quickly as possible. The hand that grasped his bare ankle was dry and cold.

"You seem in a hurry."

"I'm expected back home." He was angry with himself; he owed this uncouth stranger no explanation for his movements.

"Aren't you going in the wrong direction?" The man smiled, revealing small, pebble teeth. "I'll walk with you."

Toran felt trapped. He knew that the man sensed something unusual, and was determined to find out what it was. He couldn't let him, but didn't have the strength to resist.

"Look here," he began, but the stranger stood up and caught him by the arm. The grip felt that it was bruising his flesh, but he was so overcome with weakness, he couldn't defend himself.

"May I help?"

It was Michael. He stood, his back to the sea, ash blonde hair brilliant against his pale skin, as the sun slipped out from behind the cloud and shone fully on him. Toran felt the fingers round his arm dig deeper and, with sudden energy, he shook himself free. The man never lost his smile, but his eyes flashed in anger, and he did not look at Michael.

"So kind, but I think I'll be getting along. You never quite know when the weather will turn."

He was gone, walking down the cliff path at great speed until he was lost from sight. Toran gazed after him for a while until he could see him no more, then turned away.

"I can't tell you how glad I was that you arrived, Michael…" he began, but the words fell into empty air, and were lost in the echoes of gulls' cries, and the sound of waves.

Chapter 20

Toran reached the bush, which gleamed brighter than ever in the sunshine, and made his way to the top of the path, where he paused to gaze down at the sight below. He felt like a visitor from another time and place: the figures could have been from an old story book, or a painting of a distant age. He could not hear their voices, so silent was the scene, like a mime, and they moved with a fluid grace across the grass as the children went about their tasks. Toran marvelled as he watched them, intent upon their work, and he thought of his own misjudgement, and Edward's generosity of spirit.

He made his way down, and walked across to admire their handiwork. As he drew closer, he saw that there was a shallow cave in the cliff, and that it had already been transformed into a rough shelter for the lamb, with grass on the floor and what looked like an attempt at a rather lopsided manger, which the children had filled with straw. Now they were busy sawing wood, which they had started to put up as protection at the entrance of the cave, leaving a small entrance space. Edward smiled at him, but everyone was so absorbed in the work, they didn't pause in what they were doing. It was a touching sight, and the rhythm of their labour seemed in tune with the day, a part of the wide panorama which enfolded them. Who was he to question its deeper purpose?

The shepherds had disappeared and Solace and the lamb were nowhere to be seen, but Simon, Catherine and Ellen stood watching. Simon came over to greet his father.

"We're not needed here, as you can see."

"I hadn't noticed the cave before. How did you find it?"

"David pointed it out to us. They see everything, those

shepherds."

"Where are they? I saw them as I came down the cliff path."

"They seem to follow instincts that baffle me." Simon took his father by the arm. "But I've something I want to show you; the cave isn't the only thing we hadn't noticed. I warn you, it's a bit of a distance."

Intrigued, Toran followed as Simon led the way along the side of the cliff face. They were walking much further than he had anticipated, as though the arena expanded even as they crossed it, and the nature of the cliffs appeared to be changing as they went, for they were getting lower and crumbling a little. At last, Simon paused and turned to his father.

"Here's the place. What do you make of this?"

"However did you find it?"

"I wasn't needed, so I went for a stroll. I wanted to see how far the arena stretched, but it still seemed to continue far into the distance, and I couldn't make out where it came to an end. Then I stumbled on this."

Toran gazed for several minutes before replying.

"It looks like the remnants of a wall, and it must have been massive going by the size of the foundations and the rocks that are still standing."

"That's what I think, but it seems impossible. Why should anyone build a wall here, in front of the cliffs?"

"Could it be so ancient that it was built before these cliffs were formed?" Toran shivered.

"Oh, Dad!"

"There's more than that, Simon. I think it extended way beyond this place, farther than we could imagine. Without realising what we were doing, we must have crossed it many times."

"Surely we'd have noticed?"

"I've found you." Dinitra stood before them, smiling. They hadn't heard her approach and were startled.

"Look what we've discovered!" burst out Simon.

"Ah, yes. This arena holds many mysteries."

"But was it a wall?" Simon persisted. "I can't fathom it out."

"Not everything needs an answer straight away. A quick answer can be the wrong one. Whatever it was, it won't be needed now."

"But how…? Simon urged.

Dinitra shook her head.

"Your father looks tired. He needs rest." She held out her hand to Toran. "Come."

He took it gratefully, and allowed her to lead him across the grass like a child, whilst Simon walked beside them, and she took him back close to where the children sat chatting, having finished their labours, and helped him sit down. It was warm and sheltered where he sank to the ground, and he felt the tension in his chest ebbing as he watched the sea, and the waves breaking around the island. The gulls called to him from overhead to soothe his thoughts, and he lay on the grass and closed his eyes.

"Grandpa." Edward knelt beside him, touching his shoulder. He must have fallen asleep. "Everyone's gone to eat."

"I must've dropped off; I only lay down for a few moments." He struggled to haul himself up. "I'll come now."

"We can wait a few minutes, there's no hurry." The boy made himself comfortable. "The kids from the village, they've been a real help." His tone of voice was deliberately casual, and Toran smiled.

"I was wrong there. It was a great idea and they worked

like beavers."

"Kids can be like that."

"You're right. Sometimes, they just need a chance. We all do."

"Even you?"

"Especially me."

"Even Michael?"

"Now, there's a question. What do you think?"

"He doesn't need a chance."

"Because he is a chance, for all of us," thought Toran, and felt a sudden flash of understanding.

They sat for a few moments, enjoying being together, not wanting to make a move, until Edward spoke again.

"Have you noticed, Grandpa, the lamb? It's so tiny, and the shepherds say it won't grow any bigger. Will it die?"

"Oh no, not now you've made a shelter."

"But animals always grow!"

"I don't know. Don't you think this lamb seems different somehow?"

"It's a pity Solace can't speak. He knows."

"Ah, that's a very wise and clever dog, like the shepherds are wise too. We'll have to trust them." He took Edward's hand. "Now, let's go and eat. I bet we're both ravenous!"

After rest and refreshment, Toran felt strong enough to walk back down to the village. They had said farewell to David and Philip, who had reappeared earlier with Solace and the lamb to join them for the meal. Solace had run over and greeted him with such love that Toran felt tears start to his eyes, but the dog stayed with the shepherds and the lamb when they left. Now he looked at the children, talking and laughing as they went, and smiled with pleasure. The day had passed with nothing to break the children's tranquility, and the two he'd been concerned about had joined in

124

everything with obvious delight.

It was late afternoon, and the air was full of summer melodies, so that the climb down seemed like a celebration as the children chatted, and the adults walked in quiet contentment. Toran wished he could hold this moment of harmony and hope throughout the days ahead, an oasis of unblemished peace, where all creation seemed concordant and nothing marred the minutes. In the distance, the summit of the island was brushed with sunlight, and the star hung high above in pale isolation.

As they approached the village some time later, they became aware of a hubbub of noise and, curious and surprised, they hurried to the main street. To their astonishment, they found it filled with crowds of people standing in groups, talking earnestly.

"Whatever's going on?" Catherine looked perturbed.

"We'll take all the children home with us," said Ellen, concerned that something out of the ordinary might frighten or upset them. "You stay behind, Dad. We'll see you later." Toran nodded gratefully.

"What's happening here?" he asked the priest, who came over to him, a smile of relief on his face.

"I'm so glad to see you. I'm mystified where all these people have come from; I hardly recognise anyone. They seem to have heard about the strange event the other night and think it was some kind of omen or message."

"Omen?"

"They're afraid, yet at the same time there seems to be a stirring of hope; as if, in some way they believe that the very skies are rebelling against the threats to our fragile peace. They want to be part of that movement of hope."

"Something is evolving far beyond our comprehension."

"I agree. And there's a fair-haired woman, tall and unusual, who appeared a while ago, as if she's here for a purpose."

"I've seen her. She's very striking, isn't she." Toran hesitated. "The star?"

The priest looked up to the sky and shook his head.

"I don't know, but it seems like part of an unfolding pattern, of which we're a tiny part. What have you been searching for, Toran? You've found it, haven't you?"

"I'm not sure, but I didn't find it; I was led to it."

"And the tides - have you noticed the tides. How can it be?"

"I don't know, but it's all connected in some way, of that I'm sure."

"Even the waves…" murmured the priest. The two men stood for a few moments, lost in thought. "I'm going to ask if anyone would like to go to the church, or come to the hall for a cup of tea. I've a feeling you've something else to do. I'll see you later."

Toran walked down the street towards the sea, nodding and smiling at people as he went. He felt a surge of anticipation and hope. In the distance, he saw the tall, graceful figure standing on the top of the sand dunes, gazing out to the horizon. She didn't turn as he approached.

"The island rose from the depths in a distant age. It is seen by multitudes, but understood by few. There are many ways to climb to its summit."

"I don't understand. No-one ever goes to the island."

"Ah, that doesn't matter." Dinitra turned and smiled at him. "You are part of something which is stirring right across the globe. You are doing what you've been called to do."

"It seems so little, so insignificant. And my ideas turned out to be foolish dreams."

Dinitra shook her head.

"Oh no, a desire to provide sanctuary for others is never foolish." She paused. "Do you still have strength, Toran?"

"I think I do."

"There is one more task you have to face which will take all of that strength."

Toran looked towards the island, imagining it surging up from the seabed to stand alone, a lost kingdom hidden from sight through countless tides and seasons.

"I'll do my best," he said.

Abiding With Moving Waters

The River flowed in crystal currents, whilst season upon season passed in far other lands, but no-one came to marvel at its wide waters, and nothing stirred upon the plain except the whisper of grasses. In the distance, the glaciers hung suspended, their icy breasts locked in hidden memory. The mountains were empty and motionless, but the River foamed like forgotten seas, and the Tree was carved in stillness as the breeze blew amongst its branches.

Nathan and Rachel stood together by the edge of the dwellings, watching the star.

"Do you understand the ancient script on its surface, Nathan?"

"Only a little. That star has travelled from realms beyond our comprehension and carries with it story upon story from deep within creation. But I feel that the time is approaching for the final gathering. Do not ask me more, for it is a mystery we cannot fathom now."

"Galen and Anna?" Rachel's voice was filled with longing.

"Like Hedron, I believe they will be a part of that final consummation."

Rachel took her brother's hand.

"I will be patient."

"Nathan has a great wisdom and compassion." Hedron had joined them, and he slipped his arms through theirs and looked at the star. "For the moment, we continue with the rhythm of our lives, but the star is drawing closer and, when the hour comes, we will be ready."

"Be ready?" whispered Rachel.

"For the time when the Counsellors speak to all our people, and we take, at last, the journey back to the Tree."

The priest stood by the harbour wall, staring out to sea. The island was drenched with sunset light, its summit a halo of crimson. Each day, he watched at this hour, looking for the return of those five pilgrims, ready to welcome them and take them home.

At last he sighed, and set off back towards the village. As he passed the graveyard, he paused to look over the low but sturdy wall at the place where the man had been buried. It was on the very edge of the enclosure, in a barren spot well away from the other graves, and he remembered how the people had given a groan as the two young men started to pile the soil on top of the coffin, and how hard they had beaten it down. No earthly power could undo that burial but, before the final convergence came, the chasm would open one last time.

The priest stood for many minutes, lost in contemplation and, as he pondered, into his head came an image from far away, where another man gazed at the island and prayed for strength.

Chapter 21

They had lain huddled together under the table for a long time. No-one said what they all knew, that it was a pathetic gesture; the flimsy structure would offer no protection if an attack came. At last, Ethan spoke, his voice hoarse with tension and uncertainty.

"The planes must have just been flying over to another location, but they made such a noise, it sounded as though hell itself was being let loose on us."

"I've never heard such a din, but it wasn't what it seemed. There were no sirens, nothing." Shayrath went and looked out of the window. "The street's quiet, there's no sign of anything wrong."

"I'm going to my bed," said their mother, "I'm exhausted. I'd rather die there than spend a moment longer under that table."

Her sons nodded, and Shayrath took her arm as she walked to the bottom of the stairs. Ethan switched on a lamp, and waited for his brother to return.

"Shall we chat for a while? I don't feel ready for sleep."

"Neither do I. I'll make us a drink, then we can talk."

For a while they sat in silence, holding the steaming mugs, lost in thought. It was Ethan who spoke first, struggling to express his feelings.

"I don't understand. What I saw on the mountain, why you're carving that tree. Are they linked in any way? Nothing makes sense."

"I've no answers, Ethan, only more questions. Where are all these strangers coming from? Who are they? And, I agree, why did I feel so compelled to start working on the tree?"

"What we're doing seems so irrelevant, pointless. Yet the gypsies? They obviously know things that are hidden from us. How did they travel here so quickly when it took me days?"

Shayrath shook his head.

"I think they're hinting at something we can't grasp yet, some unfolding pattern. It started in a small way, but it's growing and spreading amongst the peoples. I believe there is hope."

Ethan yawned.

"Now, I've completely lost you. Let's get some sleep. It's almost dawn, and we need to be up early."

The market square was full of people. The brothers had expected to find an atmosphere of fear and panic after the previous evening, but no-one mentioned the planes; instead, the crowds were gathering with good humour and patience, some carrying candles, others flowers, and several musicians had arrived with their instruments, and were playing a melody that brought smiles to the faces of those nearby. People of every age were there and, contrary to custom, the different races walked together, a melting pot of faiths which made up their country.

One figure caught Shayrath's attention: tall, with skin of ebony, he walked amongst the crowds, a part of them yet distinguished by his long, black hair and upright stature, his natural dignity. The man must have sensed he was being observed, for he turned to meet Shayrath's eyes and smiled with such understanding that Shayrath felt almost shy, overcome by a mixture of sudden pleasure and bewilderment. He touched Ethan's arm.

"Let's go to the barn. We're not needed here."

"I thought there'd be uproar. This is the last thing I expected to find."

"We got it wrong. The planes have no significance."
"I agree. We need to speak to the gypsies again."

They walked along the river for some time, leaving the town behind, so absorbed in conversation that they didn't notice when they branched off in the wrong direction and took another path. The ground was still dry and dusty, with no signs of vegetation, just the occasional stark tree standing alone, but the sun shone and the brothers enjoyed its touch on their faces, and the sound of bird song. It took a little while before they realised they'd lost their route.

"However did we do that!" exclaimed Ethan.

"Talking too much! I'm sure we'll come across something familiar soon but, I must admit, at the moment I don't recognise anything. Let's just keep going; we're sure to see the barn soon." They walked quickly, becoming increasingly puzzled and annoyed with themselves for making such a careless mistake. "I thought I knew every inch of this area," said Shayrath half an hour later, as they peered ahead for a sign of the barn. "Look, there's some rocks over there. Why don't we have a quick rest and take our bearings."

"Good idea." Ethan was growing tired and welcomed the thought of a respite.

They sat in the sunshine, relaxing for a moment in the peace of their surroundings, putting to the back of their minds how they would find their way onto the right path.

"Have you noticed?" Shayrath was staring at where the stones stretched along until they disappeared from sight. "You'd almost think those had been placed there deliberately."

"Must be the result of some geological event lost in the past. I've never heard anyone mention it though. It's strange." Ethan shrugged. "I suppose we'd better get moving."

"You've found a good resting place. May I sit with you?"

The brothers spun round, startled. They'd heard no-one approaching and it had never occurred to them that someone might find this deserted spot. Standing before them, the man was an even more impressive figure than he'd looked in the market square. His skin was smooth and flawless, and his dark hair fell thickly to his shoulders. The eyes, warm and brown, shone in the sunlight.

"Please do. We're just being lazy before we move on." Shayrath felt almost shy again in the presence of this stranger, at a loss what to say. He tried to gather his manners.

"This is my brother, Ethan. I'm Shayrath."

The stranger nodded and held out both his hands to clasp those of the brothers.

"I have come a long way to find you and your people."

"Who are you?" whispered Shayrath.

"I am Seran. Now I have found you, shall we walk together to the barn."

"Have you come to join the gypsies?" Ethan's voice trembled. "Tell us what's going on!"

The man sat for a few moments, gazing along the stones stretching into the distance and, when he spoke, his words resonated, but they did not answer Ethan's question.

"There is so much in this world that is not understood, not reckoned with. Life's brief sojourn should be sacred, but it is a fragment in creation; many forget this, and imagine that their power and strength will last beyond their allotted time."

"But how can things change? People are terrified there'll be a great war, that no-one can prevent it, and the earth, already so damaged by what we've done, will be destroyed." Ethan was almost pleading. "What my brother's been attempting in the barn can have no significance. He's been fooled into thinking that what he's doing will make a difference."

Seran looked to where the star hung high above them.

"You must not despair, Ethan. Your brother has answered a call, and you have come down from the mountain to join him. Unnoticed, quietly, things have been changing for a long time."

"That's what Shayrath believes. Do you really think there won't be another war?" Ethan shook his head in bewilderment.

"You walked on the mountainside. What you saw then is carried as hope in the hearts of countless people."

"But those in power? In the end, they always turn to violence."

"Until now they have not had the courage to imagine another way. That is why we have travelled so far to find you. The seasons across the earth have been unsettled, but now is the time for healing."

"If only," whispered Shayrath.

"Have faith. As a river grows wider when it draws near to the sea, so those seeking peace and harmony find their voice."

"And the rulers?" Ethan still sounded doubtful.

"Hatred can be turned away," murmured Seran, "and manipulation and subjugation be transformed into repentance."

"I long to believe you," said Shayrath, "but I still don't understand how carving an ancient tree can make any difference to anything, although I'm driven to do it."

"You are part of the river's current, and your task is nearly finished." Seran stood up and, without hesitation, stepped over the stones. "Come, let us go to the barn together."

Chapter 22

In the great cities across the globe, in towns and villages, talk of war seemed to be receding. Perhaps it was something to do with a shifting of perceptions amongst the peoples, a feeling that there was another way, that they did not have to accept the litany of fear. Some thought it was the arrival of those from outside, the strangers who walked in the streets, moving amongst the crowds with a confidence that showed no arrogance, but exuded such a sense of quiet serenity, that it affected the way many responded, daring to hope.

It was difficult to say whether all people reacted like this, for it is not easy to discern what is in another person's heart, but the footsteps across the world were so numerous that, slowly, their beat was becoming more insistent than any voice of discord.

No-one knew where the President had gone, but he must have left because the great metal gates of the palace were permanently open, and no soldiers stood, rifles at the ready, on duty outside.

In other times, perhaps, the people would have ransacked the building, taken revenge, but now they showed no interest in such action. And even if it had crossed their minds, they were much too busy, for more and more people were arriving in the town, some in great need, others wanting to help, and there was much work to be done. Even Shayrath and Ethan's mother had left the house to see what she could do, and old enemies toiled side by side without thought for past hostilities. The swelling number of languages mixed together in an overture of voices, an impromptu music that needed no composer, such was its rhythm and harmony.

After Dinitra had left, Toran went to the village hall. So many people had arrived that the building could not contain them all, and they were spilling outside onto the grass, talking avidly. He mingled with the crowds for a while, answering questions about the dramatic sky and its appearance, but making no suggestions as to what it could have meant. Many had noticed the star and were puzzled, wondering what it might portend. Toran sensed an urgency in their speculations, and knew that these were no sensation spotters, but seekers after some much deeper truth.

After a while, he left the hall and went across to the church. As he drew close, he saw that people were standing in the graveyard, or sitting on benches and, from within, he could hear the sound of many voices. He slipped round the corner and went to sit on the seat near Jane's burial plot, and closed his eyes. He could hear the waves in the distance, and gulls flew overhead, gliding low to watch him.

"May I join you?"

Michael stood before him, the sun shining on his hair.

"I must have dropped off for a few moments!"

"You are entitled to rest."

It was difficult to believe that this was the same man who had been in the cottage such a short time ago, joining in the family meal. He seemed to have changed in some way which Toran couldn't identify. He trembled slightly as Michael sat down beside him.

"Who are you?"

"I have come a long way to find you and your people."

"But who are you?" Toran whispered again.

Michael smiled and shook his head.

"In some way, you recognised me, and took me into your home. That is enough."

"Will you stay?"

"For as long as I am needed."

"Edward?"

"He is safe."

"Where are all these people coming from? It's overwhelming. The village doesn't have the capacity to care for everyone, and more are arriving all the time. I feel at a loss to know what I should be doing, how to be of any use. When I was working as a doctor, I knew that I could help those in need. Now I seem to have been chasing illusions."

Michael looked at Toran with such compassion that tears started to his eyes, and he blinked them away, feeling foolish.

"Have faith. You responded to a call, and had the courage to begin your search alone, when all seemed impossible. A building of stone was not needed, but you found the sanctuary, and now you are helping to gather the waters of peace and the people of hope. It does not matter that you do not understand."

"Dinitra said I've one more task to undertake. I'm growing old; will I have the strength?"

Michael stood up.

"You are not alone Toran but, in the end, only you can make the choice that will face you."

He was gone, and Toran sat for a long time gazing out to sea. Voices flowed around him, every accent and all ages. The sounds soothed him and calmed his fears. The church clock struck the hour. He would return to the hall and see if he could help, then he would go home. In the morning, very early, he would walk back up the cliff path to the sanctuary.

Chapter 23

Everyone was still asleep when Toran slipped out of the front door and walked over to the church. It was a day breathing summer, and it felt as if all creation had long been stirring, celebrating the beauty of daybreak. The churchyard smelt of flowers and grasses, and hummed with early morning as he went to sit on the bench near Jane's grave. He rested there for some time, gathering strength to face the climb up the cliff path, to find the courage for whatever lay ahead.

As the clock struck six, he rose and headed for the small gate. What a different hour it seemed from when he had been resting on that same bench and seen the shepherds approaching. How he wished they would appear again now, and accompany him, but he knew that he must go alone.

The weather had changed and, as he made his way higher, the sun disappeared behind some clouds and the island was shrouded in mist. The star was a dim spot of subdued white, and the temperature had fallen. Toran shivered and paused to do up his jacket. He looked around. The landscape was deserted, as if he were the only person who ever trod that ground, and he could hear no birdsong nor see the gulls floating above him. He felt very old and tired.

He had nearly reached the first rocky outcrop on the headland, and was thinking he would pause for a rest and drink of water, when he stumbled over a loose stone and fell heavily to his knees. He cried out in pain and struggled to his feet. Gingerly he tested his legs; they were sore, but he would be able to walk. Nevertheless, he was very shaken and unsure. It was still a long way to the sanctuary, and his energy had been ebbing before he fell, so that each step had seemed more demanding. Now this careless mishap threatened to drain his confidence altogether. He limped to the rocks so that he could sit down for a few minutes and recover.

"Hello again." Toran gasped with surprise and fright; he'd been so sure that there was no-one else around. "You're out bright and early."

The man was lounging on the grass, chewing a blade as if he had all the time in the world. He looked at Toran through the sockets of his eyes, and his black hair was still plastered with oil, his skin the colour of chalk.

"You startled me."

The man smiled, showing a glimpse of small, pebble teeth. His lips were thin and moist.

"Sorry about that. Why don't you rest for a bit, take it easy?" He patted the grass beside him.

"I have to keep going." Toran could have bitten his tongue as soon as the words were spoken; he owed this stranger no explanations or excuses.

"After that tumble, it'd be foolish to set off again so soon."

"I'll just take my time; I'll be fine."

How banal he sounded, how unconvincing. He tried not to wince as he moved his leg, but the man noticed.

"You must be on a special mission, to be out alone this time of day at your age. A few minutes resting can't hurt. Nothing can be that important. Relax."

Toran strove to find his voice.

"I'll just carry on, not let the legs stiffen up."

"In that case, I'll come with you." The man smiled again. "Must be lonely on your own. I can help you. It's steep going up that path."

Toran found himself weakening, his head spinning in confusion. There was something about the man that was

139

very persuasive, and he felt troubled and uncertain. It seemed a friendly enough suggestion and he couldn't think how to refuse it without being unpleasant. There could be nothing wrong in walking a little way together; he wouldn't take him as far as the sanctuary. His knees were hurting, and he had never felt so vulnerable. He did need help. There could be no harm in accepting such an offer.

He was about to open his mouth, to give way, when he saw a dot in the distance, coming down towards him with steady intent, a tiny, solitary object, alone in all that vast panorama.

"Solace!"

The man had risen to his feet, and grasped Toran by the arm.

"Let's get going, shall we."

The eyes glittered dully, and Toran felt the malice and anger in his touch.

"Let go of me!" he cried, as strength flowed into his veins and his head cleared. He wrenched his arm free and stepped away. "I want no help from you!"

The man's eyes were lost in his skull, but he emitted such venom that, for a moment, Toran thought he was about to strike him. He prepared to defend himself, to keep fighting when, at that moment, Solace arrived and came straight to him, pressing his warm coat against Toran's legs. They remained there, motionless, and the air hung suspended around them, and the breeze ceased.

Toran would never know how long he stood, numb with anticipation. At last, in the distance, he could see the summit of the island appearing out of the mist, touched with light. At that instant, the man took a step backwards and lost his footing.

"Look out!" yelled Toran, but it was too late. The cliffs plummeted unmeasured chasms to the sea, and he had been standing dangerously close to the edge. Before Toran could move, the man had fallen to his stomach and was clutching at tufts of grass in a desperate attempt to save himself. For several appalling seconds, he watched as he slithered backwards, his face distorted with horror and disbelief, until he slid over the top with a scream of terror, and disappeared from sight.

They waited, but everything was silent. Toran grasped one of the rocks nearby and peered cautiously over the edge. No body floated on the surface, nor smallest ripple suggested that anyone had been claimed by those powerful tides.

The stranger, whoever or whatever he had been, was no more.

Chapter 24

When Toran and Solace reached the sanctuary, Toran was exhausted. He didn't know how he would have made the journey if the dog hadn't stayed by his side, whimpering encouragement from time to time. At first glance, the arena appeared deserted, and he looked around, puzzled and worried. Where were the shepherds and Dinitra, the lamb? He stood for a few moments, feeling lost and uneasy, thinking he'd made a mistake and should go home. Then he saw Michael, almost hidden by sunlight, standing far away across the arena, gazing out to sea. Toran felt his heart lifting, but he hesitated, wondering what to do. The man appeared so absorbed, it seemed wrong to approach him, yet he wanted nothing more than to go and speak with him, seek reassurance. As he stood, torn between longing and doubt, Solace nudged him gently and started to walk across the grass, pausing to look behind, checking that Toran was following him. With a surge of relief and gratitude, he stepped forward.

Michael didn't turn as they drew close, but his voice was clear.

"Do you notice a change in the island, Toran?"

Toran stared with surprise. The weather had altered again, and it was difficult to believe that the day had been dull and cold earlier; the water was turquoise, flecked with surf, and the island was turrets of silver, its peak looking different, as though it had expanded and taken on new life.

"The summit looks greener, bursting with fresh growth."

"Yes."

"I thought it must be a trick of the light."

"Or something you have not discerned before. It can take

a long time to see clearly what has been there all the time."

They stood together, watching the vista ahead. The star hung over the island, bright and clear, and the sea surged and raced towards the horizon.

"So, your task is done."

"You know." Michael nodded. "I still don't understand. That man… His death…?"

"You did not kill him, Toran; he died because he could not sway you, although he tried with all his might to do so."

"What did he want?"

"To destroy the sanctuary, but he has been defeated and is far below the very foundations of the island, where stones hold his skeleton in their grip, and barnacles blind him. His rage is ended and he has no more power."

"Was he so powerful?"

"Only when he was allowed to be so."

"But our world, it's so fractured and broken, so full of hatred and violence. How can not giving way to one man make any difference? Most people long for peace, but the powerless and innocent are always defeated, and all their tears turn to drought. It's always been the same!"

"Wrong can only be defeated by quiet resolve, not loud noise and violent action. The smallest seed of belief, rightly nurtured, can grow into a mighty gathering of hope."

Toran sighed.

"I was very afraid."

"You were right to be afraid, but you have been faithful and brave. Well done. Now, go and sleep."

While Toran lay on the warm grass, with Solace by his side, the rest of the family arrived, accompanied by many more children. Simon went straight to kneel down beside his father, and touched his brow. He looked exhausted, but he was peaceful. Ellen stood watching with concern.

"He's driven himself too hard."

"I don't think he had a choice. He'll be alright. I'll keep on checking he's okay."

The children were running around with Lachlan and Joquella, shouting and laughing, but Edward slipped away to walk across to the shelter. He paused there for a few moments, listening intently, then turned to trudge across the wide expanse of grass, small and determined, until he reached the far side where Michael still stood gazing out to sea.

"Hello, Edward. You've found me, and I've been waiting for you."

"I've been looking for you, Michael. Can I stay with you for a bit?"

The man took the boy's hand and led him across the grass to sit on some rocks a little distance away.

"I've never noticed these before," exclaimed Edward.

"It's a good place to chat and think, and we may not have another chance to do so."

For a few minutes, the two sat in companionable silence, like any father and son enjoying being together on a summer's day. Michael waited for the boy to speak first.

"I'm muddled," Edward burst out at last. "I got to the shelter before the others. They were just messing about. And I thought I heard the sound of a baby crying. I looked inside, but I couldn't make things out properly, it was quite dark inside. Then I thought I heard the lamb bleating, crying in some way, and that must've been what I heard in the first place. But I couldn't see the lamb either, and I think it's disappeared. Solace is with Grandpa, and Solace never leaves the lamb. I'm worried."

Edward had talked at such speed, and with so much emotion, that he could no longer contain himself. To his dismay, he felt tears pouring down his cheeks. He sniffed, and wiped his nose with his hand.

"Here, let's use this." Smiling, Michael held out a handkerchief and wiped away the tears. "That's a good start."

"Is the lamb safe, do you think? It never seemed to grow."

"You need not worry about the lamb. It was your idea to build the shelter, and you cannot begin to understand how many your shelter will protect, but all will be well."

"Promise me!"

"All will be well. Go to your family now, for I have to leave."

"Will I see you again?"

"Not quite like this, but you'll know when I'm nearby."

Edward stood up and, shyly, held out his hand. Michael rose, and took it, and laid his other hand on the boy's brow.

"Bless you, Edward," he said, and watched as the child walked slowly away to join his family.

Chapter 25

It was very early morning when Shayrath and Ethan set off for the barn once more. Despite the hour, when most residents would usually be sleeping, the town was ringing with activity, the square crowded, and pungent smells of cooking coming from the many fires and stalls. There was still a steady influx of people, and the whole place was transformed, its drabness vanished, its subdued monotony a distant memory. The brothers stopped to exchange greetings, accept a steaming coffee, and listen to some of the conversations going on all around them.

"Well!" said Ethan, as they finally left the crowds behind and made their way along the path by the river. "What do you make of that?"

"Extraordinary! Word has spread about that sky the other night; people believe it was some kind of omen, or message. After the fear and consternation when it happened, now there seems to be some sense of hope, a belief that things are changing."

"Do you think it's connected to what we're doing, Shayrath?"

"I couldn't say, but it feels like an unfolding pattern of which we're just a tiny part." Shayrath shook his head. "Do you think the gypsies will know?"

"If they do, they probably won't tell us." Ethan paused. "But Seran seems to understand everything, even before it's taken place."

Heads bowed, lost in thought, they walked for some time without speaking.

"I don't believe it!" exclaimed Shayrath suddenly, "We've gone off route again."

Ethan looked ahead and laughed.

"You're right, but there's the stones. I think we'll find our way to the barn with them as a landmark."

"I agree. And the way we went with Seran was much nicer than the usual path we've always taken, so it's a lucky mistake." Shayrath stared with increasing interest as they drew closer. "You know, I still believe that these rocks were put there for a purpose. Do you think they could be remnants of an old wall?

"No! Why should anyone in their right mind build a wall here! It'll be what I said – the consequence of some distant geological event. Why don't we take the opportunity to sit down for a few moments."

"Okay, but don't let's stay long, it's getting chilly." Shayrath glanced up: the sun had disappeared, and the star was barely visible. He shivered and did up his jacket before perching on the stones next to his brother.

"You've found a good resting place. May I join you?"

The brothers jumped with surprise, and stumbled to their feet.

"You!" Ethan exclaimed.

It was the same man: tall, head disconcertingly small for his body, black hair sleeked back as if for some old photograph, white cheeks pulled tautly across his face. He was dressed in the identical dark suit, with a red shirt and tie.

Ethan fought to quell his rising sense of panic. He saw Shayrath watching the man uneasily, wondering what was going on.

"Yes, I get around, like to explore, meet people." The man smiled briefly, revealing small, pebble teeth. His lips were thin and moist.

"Well, hope you have a good day," said Shayrath, trying to sound friendly, but help his brother, who looked pale and shaken. "We're just off, I'm afraid."

"Wait a moment!" The man grasped Shayrath by the arm. "Perhaps I could come with you."

Shayrath tried not to show his distaste. He stepped back, pulling his arm free. Ethan was still silent and rooted to the ground.

"That's not possible. We only came out for a stroll and need to hurry back."

"Curious time of morning for a stroll." The man smiled again. "I've a feeling you were heading in the other direction from the town. Must be something important to get you out so early."

"It's nothing, just a bit of woodwork." Shayrath could have bitten his tongue the moment the words were out. They owed this stranger no explanations. Ethan looked dismayed.

"I'll certainly come with you then; I'm quite an expert with wood. I can help you. There must be a lot of work to do if you're going at this hour."

Into Ethan's head flashed images of the carnage in that far distant town, of people dying beside him even as they fled. Could it be that his memory was playing tricks on him? Had he imagined that this man had fired a gun? He sounded so reasonable now that it was difficult to think clearly. If he were violent, a murderer, he wouldn't be here in the countryside on a summer morning, chatting about woodwork. He pulled himself together and cleared his throat.

"That's kind of you, but we don't need any help. We already have it."

"Ah." The man's eyes glittered from deep within the sockets. "That's nice to know, but an extra pair of hands is always useful."

The brothers stood in paralysed silence. Shayrath was bewildered as to how Ethan could have met this stranger

148

before. The man was very persistent, and his startling appearance made him recoil, yet it seemed unkind to deny someone such a simple request. Ethan could say nothing more. He felt weak, out of control, lethargy creeping into his bones like a sluggish tide. He would leave his brother to take control of the situation,

Shayrath knew he was being left to make a decision. His mind was foggy, and he tried to think rationally. What harm could it do if this man came with them some of the way? They wouldn't allow him to go with them to the barn; they'd find an excuse to get rid of him.

"Well, just a short..." he began, when they heard the sound of footsteps on the dry ground.

"Great." The response was eager. "We won't go over these stones though. I know a quicker path to the barn."

Before either brother could ask how this stranger knew about the barn, they saw a figure coming towards them through the trees. It was Matthew. Relief swept over them as he came to stand on the other side of the rocks.

"Ah, here you are," he said pleasantly.

"We're about to leave." The man was locked in tension and determination, and he didn't look at Matthew. "It's already decided; we're going another way."

Matthew inclined his head..

"In that case, I'll return to my work," he said. He smiled at the brothers. "I may see you later."

He was gone before either had time to speak, and they longed to call him back, but they stood rigid, unable to find their voices. The visit had been so fleeting, it was difficult to believe he'd been there. The man caught Ethan's arm.

"We'll be off then. No time to waste."

The three men stood as in a tableau, and nothing else stirred for unbroken minutes, until Ethan uttered a sudden cry as he felt energy flowing back into his veins.

"Let go of me!" he roared, and wrenched his arm from the grip of the other man. Shayrath rushed to his brother's side. His head had cleared and he saw with a shudder the face of the stranger. It had changed, and the hollow eyes glittered with such venom that he was aghast. How did they so nearly follow him?

"We're not going your way. You can't come with us."

The man took a step backwards, seeming to shrink even as they watched. They were about to leave, step over the rocks, when Shayrath stiffened.

"Don't move!"

The snake was coming towards them, gliding along the side of the stones. Its eyes seemed to stare with deadly intent at the stranger, and the man gave a howl of fear and started to run. Shayrath and Ethan watched in horror as the creature followed him. The man fell to his belly and crawled along the ground for a few moments, then pulled himself up again and continued fleeing. As he disappeared into the distance, they saw him fall again, and this time they didn't see him rise. A few moments later they heard a shriek, then all was silent.

"What shall we do?" Ethan was shaking..

"We can't just leave, however unpleasant he was."

They ran to the place where they'd seen the stranger fall, looking around cautiously in case the snake was still close by. There was no sign of the creature, nor could they see any trace of the man. The land was flat and open, with only the odd withered tree to break the monotony. If he were still alive and able to move, they would spot him. He had vanished.

"There's nothing we can do," said Shayrath. "I just hope that's the end of it."

Ethan scanned the area once more.

"I think it is." He saw his brother staring around, looking

anxious. "And of the snake."

Without speaking, they walked back to the stones and crossed over, hurrying to make up for lost time, for they were both anxious to get to the barn and carry on with their work. After a short way, they saw the elegant figure coming towards them and their hearts lifted. Ethan ran to greet him.

"I was expecting you; I thought we could walk together again," said Seran.

"We're so pleased to see you," began Shayrath, "we met this man…"

"I'd seen him before," whispered Ethan.

"None of that matters now." Seran's voice was firm. "You weren't swayed by him, and you are coming to the barn. You have been brave and faithful. Well done."

"Ethan thinks he won't appear again?"

Seran's voice was rich and full of reassurance.

"Whoever, or whatever he was, he is no more. Now, let's hurry, for the others are waiting for you."

The gypsies were sitting around the fire when the brothers arrived, sipping their sweet smelling brew.

"Come and join us," called the eldest, "have a rest. We shall be moving on soon and may not see you again."

"Where are you going?" Ethan looked sad as he and Shayrath took the proffered goblets and joined their circle.

"Difficult to say," said the youngest.

"You're not gypsies are you," said Ethan, "I've always been puzzled why you were alone. Who are you? Please tell us before you go."

The youngest man smiled.

"We're many things: seekers, travellers, gift bearers, holders of mystery."

"And the star?" It was Shayrath who spoke.

"Ah, yes. That too."

They fell silent, and the brothers knew they could ask no more questions. The flames licked the wood lazily, and the old piebald horse grazed nearby. Ethan sighed.

"We'd better get on," he said, and the three men nodded and held out their hands.

Inside the building, the lamps cast their shadowy glow in the centre whilst, all around the edges, darkness hung in silent folds. Matthew and Josiah were kneeling by the tree, deep in concentration. The brothers gasped.

"How've you managed all that work in such a short time!" Shayrath was perturbed. Had he failed at his task after all?

Matthew smiled at him.

"You'll never know how much you've achieved, Shayrath. We've been waiting for you. Let's work together now, and complete what must be done."

The brothers nodded and dropped to their knees beside the other two men. Shayrath ran his hand along the wood.

"It's so fine," he said, "so majestic. Ever since that day we found it as boys, it's always had some hidden power."

After the disturbing events of the morning, the brothers were relieved and contented to work, and the next hours were some of the happiest either could remember. No-one spoke, but the steady rhythm and quiet companionship soothed them, giving them peace and, as the day moved into evening, and their labour was almost done, the tree seemed to breathe, as if new roots were forming, and its forgotten planting stirred within its body. At last, they stood and gazed at what they'd done, and knew that the task was finished.

"It's time for you to go now," said Matthew. "We'll see you in the morning." Josiah nodded.

"I'll come with you and taste the air."

When they stepped outside once more, the caravan and old piebald horse were no longer there, and the last embers of fire glowed in the empty space. Ethan paused.

"That's sad," he whispered, and said no more.

As the barn disappeared into the distance, and Josiah left them, the brothers walked on towards the town. Silence spread all around, so that both land and sky seemed suspended in anticipation, and it felt as if they were the only people in the whole globe, with just the star for company, to guide them home.

Chapter 26

When Toran walked out of his front door the next morning, the place was alive with activity. Many more had arrived overnight, and the villagers had offered their homes and hearts to welcome them. Although his cottage was full to brimming with his children and grandchildren, the family were helping in other ways. He saw Simon, Catherine and Ellen pouring out drinks, and putting piles of rolls on the tables. Many incomers had brought food with them, and this was added to the communal supplies. The shopkeeper had opened his doors, and children ran to and from the store with baskets of bread and fruit, eager to be part of the sense of excitement and anticipation.

Toran strolled over to the church, where the priest was laying out tables in the graveyard, and the doors of the ancient building were held back so that sunlight could stream in, accompanying the many people who entered. Birdsong filled the air, and the scent of freshly mown grass assailed his senses.

"This movement is beyond anything we imagined, Toran, when we spoke before. And people are still pouring into the village!"

"It's what you said: an onset of hope, the longing for peace."

"The other night, when everyone was so afraid and took shelter in the church. Something changed."

"The people thought it presaged some terrible disaster but, instead, they started to notice the star. The thought of its journey across unknown galaxies to reach here touched something long buried in so many; they don't know why, but they feel it's come to offer a new way." Toran paused.

"Does that sound like the ramblings of an old man?" The priest shook his head.

"What you're trying to say is difficult to express in words. Most people have felt powerless for so long, even though we are luckier than many in the world. Something has prompted a desire to gather rather than disperse, to help rather than compete, to listen rather than talk. If such feelings become a flood, then love may overcome hatred after all."

"And everyone would find sanctuary," whispered Toran.

The two men stood together for a few moments, deep in thought.

"Another strange thing," said the priest, "do you know how many languages there are in the world?"

Toran looked puzzled.

"Well over six thousand, I think. Why do you ask?"

"This is an insulated and tucked away little place, yet in these last hours I've heard many languages which I don't recognise, and a mingling of voices that need no interpretation. What can that mean?"

Toran climbed the cliff path alone. He knew he would soon be followed, but he wanted a few quiet moments to discern and reflect, prepare himself for whatever lay ahead. The star was hanging lower in the sky, seeming to watch him as he walked. The sea was flecked with white and, after a while, he stopped to look down at the currents sweeping across the mouth of the bay. Puzzled, he stared more closely, trying to check that what he thought he'd glimpsed was not just his imagination.

He shook his head in disbelief. Not only did the island appear closer but, every now and then, he caught a flash of huge rocks just below the surface, which seemed to stretch from there to the mainland. Is that what the falling tides had been about: to reveal that long ago the land formation had been different, and the island had once been accessible on foot? The more he gazed, the greater was his conviction that he hadn't made a mistake. He must reach the sanctuary as quickly as possible, and ask Michael or Dinitra if he were deluded.

Solace was waiting for him when he reached the bush and, together, they walked down the familiar path. There was no sign of David and Philip, but he saw Dinitra standing on the far side of the arena, looking out to sea, and he went over to her, the dog close by his side.

"I'm glad you've come early." Dinitra smiled in greeting. "I've been waiting for you."

"I wanted to arrive first, to be ready. Please tell me what's happening!"

"Happening?"

"I'm sure I spotted something, just beneath the waves. The tide's falling again, so soon it should become clearer."

"What is it you think you see?"

"Was there once some kind of natural causeway between the island and sanctuary, which disappeared long ago in the deeper waters, but now's being exposed?"

"You're seeing creation through a different lens, Toran, through other eyes."

"So it was there, and can be crossed again!"

"Yes, if it's discovered, it can be crossed."

"And the garden on the summit of the island, am I imaging its beauty, the way it seems to grow even as I watch?"

"What do you think?"

"I can see it, but is what I'm witnessing from a distant past, or is it happening now?"

"The garden has always been there. It's a part of the living past and the time ahead."

"And now is the season of plenty." Michael stood beside them. "When all people may join in the feast if they wish."

He turned to leave. "I can hear the sound of countless footsteps; the sanctuary has been found, Toran, and your task done."

"Wait!" cried Toran. Dinitra touched him gently on the arm.

"You knew he must go," she said, "but you're not alone. See how low the star is. Its hour has come."

The people were pouring into the arena, gasping with awe as they arrived. Edward, Lachlan and Joquella ran over to their grandfather.

"You've no idea how many are coming, Grandpa!" cried Edward.

"The line stretches back to the village and beyond," said Simon, who had joined them. "All ages, all kinds of people, well and infirm, strangers and friends, helping each other up the path."

"It's the opposite of the vision I had from the hill that day, when I looked down on the loch," said Catherine. "I hoped there'd be another way, but I could never quite believe there would."

"The island is closer than we thought," murmured Toran, "it just seemed so far away."

"And the arena." Ellen slipped her arm into her father's. "It seems immeasurable, as if you could never reach its boundaries."

"It has none." Dinitra stood with them. "No boundaries are needed here."

Until this moment, Solace had been by Toran's side without moving, but now he nudged him and whimpered.

"He wants to show me something. Shall we go with him?"

They followed the dog along the cliff, past the spot where Simon had taken his father to see remnants of what might once have been a wall, further still, until they saw it, a winding grassy slope leading down to the sea.

"Solace!" cried Simon, "how did you find this?"

"Because he's cleverer than we are," smiled Toran. He looked around at the multitudes, standing in hushed silence as they saw the island soaring so close by. "Look, it's clear to see now what the falling tides have revealed. The island was joined to the land by a great, natural causeway, which has been submerged and forgotten through many ages." He turned to Dinitra. "What must we do now?"

"Spread the word that we can cross, and that everyone may follow."

She waited as the message rippled through the crowds, like the waves that flowed before them and, soon afterwards, a great shout went up from the people, a shout that echoed round and round in reverberations of hope. The star was starting to move away, into the higher reaches of the sky, but the sun shone with renewed energy and warmed their faces. Dinitra took Edward's hand, and held up her other arm.

"Let us go!" she cried, and the people followed her over the stones, into the abundance and shelter of the garden.

Early the next morning, Shayrath and Ethan arrived in the market square with their mother. More people than ever had gathered, and excited chatter filled the air. As they walked through, crowds of children swarmed round them, full of questions.

"Everyone thinks you know what's happening, why the star's come. It's getting brighter and closer all the time. Do you think it'll get even nearer?" The boy was obviously the spokesman, and many pairs of eyes gazed at the brothers, waiting for an answer.

"We don't know," said Shayrath, "we're walking in that direction, following its light."

"Can we come with you?"

"Everyone is welcome. Find your parents and then follow the path. You won't get lost, the way's quite clear now."

"I'll wait with the children, make sure they're safe."

Ethan looked at his mother to make sure that she really meant her offer; her transformation still amazed him.

"That's kind, Mother. Will you be alright?"

She nodded and smiled at him.

"Go on with you. We'll be close behind."

The brothers walked towards the barn, filled with a mixture of nervousness and hope.

"Whatever happens," said Ethan, "I think all our people will be safe at last, as I saw on the mountainside all that time ago. I should have understood the message and I failed, but now the river is growing wider as it draws near to the sea, as Seran said it would, and the trickle that was my doubt has joined that flood of hope."

"And those who hold the power?" murmured Shayrath.

"Perhaps they're discovering the courage to imagine another way," said Ethan.

"As Seran also said." Shayrath smiled. "We must hurry."

Ethan laughed. "Let's run, as we used to do as boys."

They stood in the barn, their hearts pounding. It lay on the floor, gigantic in size, breath-catching in its undying power, and the tree that had died so it could be transformed was present in the ancient grooves, and air of broken majesty.

"I've never seen one like it," whispered Ethan, "it seems so much larger even than the tree it was carved from. What a task you started, Shayrath, all alone with no-one close by to offer help."

"What must we do now?" Shayrath stood at a loss "I've

never thought about what's to be done once the work was finished."

Ethan shook his head.

"Nor have I, but surely we can't leave it here?"

In their consternation, they hadn't heard Matthew's approach, and they greeted him with exclamations of relief.

"Oh, Matthew, what must we do now? The wood's impossible to move."

"It will be moved, and taken out of here, across the fields to the place beyond, then we'll raise it up until it stands high above everything else."

"Can so few really…" began Shayrath, but Matthew held up his hand.

"Listen!"

They heard a sound, as of distant running waters and, as it came closer, the great barn doors opened, and it was the people's voices that were like the singing of waters, and their footsteps that echoed with the murmur of the breeze. Matthew stood before them as they gazed in astonishment at what lay on the ground. He pointed to a pile of sturdy ropes.

"These ropes need to be attached securely to the wood, so that it can be taken back to its rightful home. Now we are all gathering, the task can be completed."

Shayrath and Ethan were the first to respond, joined swiftly by many helpers, and they started to tie the ropes to the wood, pulling the knots tight so that they would hold.

"Why," breathed one of the women, "it's in the shape of a cross. Whatever can it mean?"

"Pull!" cried Matthew, and Josiah, who stood next to the brothers, bent over and seized the end of one of the ropes.

"Pull!" he roared. They struggled with every fibre in their being, but the wood did not move.

"Help us!" cried Shayrath to Seran who stood watching

silently, but he shook his head. For whatever reason, he would not join them. The weight of the cross was beyond all calculation and, despite their combined willingness and strength, it did not stir. "Please!" cried Shayrath and, at that moment, he felt the rope tugging in his hands and the wood trembled. A shout went up from the people, and Seran raised his arms and gave a great cry of triumph.

They dragged the wood out of the barn, and started to take it over the fields. The landscape was changing before their eyes. In front of them lay an immense plain and, across it, ran a wide river, sparkling under the light of the star. As they pulled, more and more people joined to take hold of the ropes and help and, when there was no more room, the growing multitudes walked behind. When they reached the centre of the plain, Seran raised his hand again.

"Bring it upright. Have faith, it can be done."

"It's not possible," muttered Ethan, "surely it'll fall."

"We'll have to try and force the base into the ground," said Shayrath, "and trust that it'll hold. We must do as Seran says."

Many pulled on the ropes, whilst others pushed with their hands, and then held the wood fast, as those strong enough struggled to make it secure. At last it stood upright, towering over them, its arms stretched out in invitation and, as they stared in astonishment, it seemed to rise ever higher, and from its base they saw great roots springing which sank into the soil even as they watched. The shape of the wood was changing, the arms spreading wider and wider, as though reaching out in embrace and, as they gazed in awe, the arms multiplied into great branches that arched over the multitude, its green boughs parting to reveal the star.

Shayrath stood and wept, and saw that those around him were weeping too. He wiped his face as a sudden wind swept across the plain and dried their tears, and then was gone.

"The Tree!" he breathed, "of course, it's the Tree."

The star was moving into the higher reaches of the sky, and the sun shone down on them with increased light. Far across the plain, he could see more people arriving, coming down a path from another way. They moved with an unusual grace, a choreography of harmony and peace and, as their feet touched the grasses, they started to run.

Seran watched as they drew closer, his back to the massive trunk and, when they were not far off, he raised his arms in welcome, as the branches soared overhead, and the river sang its symphony, and the glaciers sparkled in the distance, empty of any shadow.

Gathering

The priest stood by the harbour wall staring out to sea, the villagers gathered around him. The island was swathed in light and, through the haze, they glimpsed the garden, covering the summit with greens and golds.

They saw the boat floating through the gap in the harbour walls, and knew that it had travelled unmeasured distances to reach them. The people watched until it rested just below where they stood, the water lapping against the bow. The five occupants looked tired, but their faces were alight with relief and gratitude. The priest held out his hands in welcome, as a great sigh of contentment went up from the crowd.

"You are home," he said. "We have waited for you. Now we may all return to the island together."

Hedron and Nathan were leading the people back to the plain. They passed amongst the woods, where light glanced in, along undulating pathways, and through the valley of slender trees. They followed the star and the scent of water, for there was no other way. At last, they stood looking down, mute with wonder, as they gazed at the spreading branches, the untouched fruit hanging amongst the leaves.

"You lead us, Hedron," said Nathan to the old Counsellor. "Your memory and faithfulness have led us here."

Hedron smiled and shook his head.

"The star has guided us and now, do you see, it is moving to the upper reaches of the sky so that it too may return home. Come, all our people, let us go together to the shelter of the Tree."

They followed him down the path and, when he stepped

on to the grasses, he paused and held out his arms. The people gathered in multitudes around him and lifted their arms also, then, with one heart, they started to run.

On the other side of the plain, coming down the path that led from the glacier, two figures could be seen, walking slowly. They were a little stooped but, even at this distance, it was clear that the man must once have been of an unusual height. White curls tumbled to his shoulders, and the woman's hair cascaded down her back.

Rachel stopped for a moment and took Nathan's hand.

"Could it be?" she whispered.

Nathan stared across the space for a few moments, then threw back his head with joy.

"It is Galen and Anna," he said, "returning home at last."